THE SCARLET CROSS

CHAOS CURSE BOOK 2

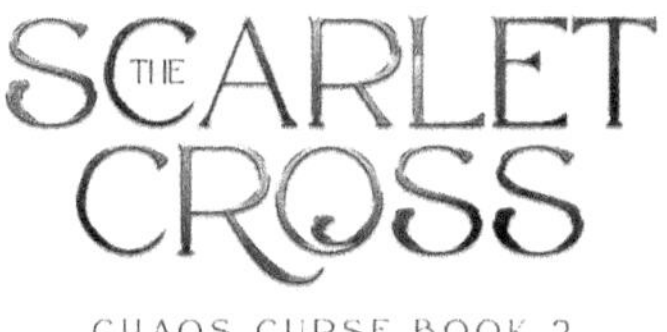

Copyright © 2024 by Kasey LeAlma

Contact info:
kasey@kaseylealma.com
www.kaseylealma.com
www.instagram.com/kaseylealma

Published by: Moon Witch Books LLC
Cover Design by: GetCovers.com
Line Editor: Lana Staux, The Fiction System, Quill Shadow Publishing
Copy Editor: Jeanine Harrell, Indie Edits with Jeanine
Formatting by: Alyssa Green, Green Spark Publishing
Proofread: Brittany Riley, Fox Tale Publishing

Ebook ISBN: 978-1-961587-03-8
Paperback ISBN: 978-1-961587-04-5
First Edition: November 2024

KASEY LEALMA

THE SCARLET CROSS

CHAOS CURSE BOOK 2

ALSO BY KASEY LEALMA

<u>Chaos Curse Series</u>

The Zodian Warrior

The Scarlet Cross

Author's Note

Thank you for picking up *The Scarlet Cross*. While writing it, it became darker than I had anticipated, but I knew it was the right direction. I just wanted to give you a heads-up about some themes and events in this book that might be sensitive or triggering for some readers.

This story includes pieces of the following:

- *Death and Loss:* Characters experience the death of loved ones and deal with grief.
- *Violence and Combat:* There are graphic descriptions and some scenes of torture.
- *Romantic and Sexual Content:* The story has a romantic and sexual scene.
- Please feel free to skim or skip if needed.

Again, thank you for choosing Ember and Luke's story.

*I want to thank my husband, Jeremy, for believing in me
and rooting for me to become rich and famous so he can
quit his day job to ride motorcycles all day.*

*And as always,
Aunt Wanda
(I hope she enjoys this!)*

Heath slid against the concrete wall with a thud, the rock torpedoes that flew by just missing him. *He's on the run.* With a deep breath, he cocked his gun and counted the seconds until he could fire back. The buzz in his pocket told him she'd called for the *third time.* He hated missing her call, but he knew what they needed to talk about and refused to have that conversation.

"Sir, the wall," someone called from behind.

Heath jumped, rolling away from the falling wall. He sprinted past the debris, trying to cut the monster off before it reached the back door of the building. He tossed a smoke bomb from his utility belt; it was laced with canceling herbs that would subdue the target. Thankfully, he already had a mask on. He came out of the smoke ready to fire. The balaur spawn was leaning against the back wall, wheezing, close to the door but not yet there.

"Stop," Heath yelled, and at the same time, a rose

sprang out of the ground, piercing through the concrete and growing as tall as both men.

The demon touched the flower and smiled. "Now you'll pay."

He lifted his hands, and spiked stones rose from the ground, flying straight for him.

Heath covered his face and crouched behind a car, avoiding the projectiles, but a few hit his shoulder. He grunted at the force, but the projectiles dissolved into dirt on impact. *The smoke's working.* He craned his Beretta at the monster and fired a few rounds.

The spawn raised the slab of concrete, shielding himself from the bullets, and then more stone icicles soared through the air only to dissolve into dirt mid-flight.

Heath's men were finally catching up.

"You're surrounded," he yelled, but the supernatural grimaced.

The structure shook.

"Sir, he's going to level it down," a soldier shouted as he came into the area.

"He's going to kill us all," another one yelled.

"Not until we have him," Heath hissed. *I need this win.* "The smoke is working. He's losing his powers."

"If he wants to bring down the building, we can help," a new recruit shouted, throwing a round ball toward the demon.

"No," Heath yelled, watching in horror as the tiny explosive landed.

He turned, and it flashed before the concussion hit him.

Heath blinked awake, the scent of gasoline overwhelming him. He coughed, pulling himself off the ground. Debris fell to the floor as he climbed to his feet. The building groaned and beams snapped. *We have to get out of here.* He searched the area for his men and checked the pulses of the ones he found. Only one was alive. He dragged him in the direction of the exit.

A beam blocked their path, and he laid the guy down by it. He tried to lift it, but his strength was gone.

"I can help," someone said below him.

Heath whipped his gun out, pointing it at the monster. "You're the reason this happened."

The demon trapped under electrical wires chuckled. His leg was twisted at an odd angle. "My power might be dimmed, but I can help you, if you help me."

Heath didn't know what to do. He wouldn't help a balaur spawn, but he was running out of time. The whole building would collapse any moment.

He nodded. "Clear the doorway first."

The man grunted and closed his eyes to concentrate before the beam lifted slowly off the ground. It fell with a thud a few feet away. The walls shook, but the opening was cleared.

He groaned, "Now the wires."

Heath lifted his fallen comrade and hobbled to the opening. "I'll be back."

He walked through the doorway. Sunshine streamed

down on his face. The monster began screaming as he exited the parking garage.

"Fucking liar!"

The pillars gave way, sending Heath and the soldier flying through the air. They landed on the grass several feet from where the building came crashing down.

Heath climbed the steps to Makani's apartment. It had been a grueling day, and it wasn't over. Makani was going to break up with him. He had fifteen missed calls.

He'd been the only survivor of the building disaster. The man he carried to safety had never regained consciousness, and the doctors declared him brain dead. His mother was furious. He'd gone in with fifteen soldiers under him to take care of a small group of supernaturals. None of the monsters had been captured unless they counted the one who died by being smashed beneath the building. And of course, his mother did not.

He was exhausted. On the outside of the apartment door, he raised his hand to knock when he heard her sobs. "Makani!" He twisted the handle, barging in. "Are you okay?"

She sat in the middle of the floor, wrapped in a blanket, with tears streaming down her beautiful face.

He crossed the room in three strides, pulling her to him. "What's wrong?"

She sniffled. "He's gone," she said. "He's gone. Gone! They called. He's dead."

"I'm right here?" Heath said, hugging her tighter.

She was shaking.

She sobbed into his shirt, her hands gripping the fabric. She glimpsed up at him with tear-stained cheeks. No semblance of the woman he knew. "I can't have this baby without him."

He could hear the desperation in her voice.

The air shifted around him, and he stilled. Looking up, he noticed they were floating. *What the hell?* He pulled back from her, and they dropped to the ground.

Makani scrambled back from him, fearful. She whispered, "I'm sorry."

He stood frozen in the center of the room. She was balaur.

"I . . ." He couldn't finish.

He'd already reached for his concealed knife. *What the fuck am I doing?* He sheathed the blade.

Makani stood, wiping the tears from her face.

"Don't worry. I'll take care of you." Heath let loose a breath and damned his soul. "I love you."

One

EMBER

Approximately twenty-four years later . . .

My key in the lock didn't turn.

I wiggled the handle, hoping that would fix the problem, but the door didn't budge. *He really meant it.* I pulled the key out and turned on my phone's flashlight as the last of the sun's rays dimmed in the late evening sky. I checked the key to ensure it was the correct one. Which of course it was. *He's such an ass.*

"Did you lock yourself out?" Grace asked, standing a few feet behind me.

I'd picked her up on the way over for support.

"No." I stepped back.

I chose to stop by after my afternoon shift at the bank, assuming Dad would be home. However, the windows were dark, the curtains drawn shut. Either no one was here, or Dad hadn't bothered with the lights yet.

The last time I saw him was the day he told me he no

longer wanted to be my family. *I don't need or want you.* My body shivered despite the heat of September. I ran my hands up and down my arms, trying to shake off his cold, harsh words. By choosing my powers, I'd saved Hannah's life—it never occurred to me he wouldn't be able to forgive me eventually. *He only needs time to adjust to my decision.*

"Dad," I yelled. "Can you unlock the door? We need to talk." I knocked.

No answer.

I pounded harder. The wood shook under my fist, glass rattling.

I'd stopped by the house several times over the last two weeks to grab necessities, but it had always been during the times I knew Dad would not be home in order to give him that distance. The space I thought he needed. But this? This told a different story. It was weird that we hadn't spoken. He used to call like clockwork every week during college.

"This is stupid," I muttered to the awakening crickets.

I had done nothing wrong. He had to come around. My powers weren't going anywhere.

Grace climbed the steps to the porch, poking into the withered flower bed. "Isn't there a spare key around here somewhere?"

I bent down, lifting the front mat, but all I found was a key-shaped stain. "Nope." I laughed. "He must have changed the locks." I checked the aether in the house, but emptiness reverberated back to me. Grace's silver thread glittered around me. "He's not here."

The sensation of bubbly champagne hit my nose at the same time that a light flickered behind me. "Grace?" I turned, but she was nowhere in sight.

The door opened, and Grace poked her head out. "Come on," she said, standing back.

I stepped into the house. By the time I shut the front door, casting everything into darkness, Grace had made it to the stairs. I followed her.

Grace tilted her head and asked, "What is it you need to get?"

I shrugged. "Extra clothes." *What I really want isn't here.*

We came to the landing and headed to my room. I stepped inside, my eyes slowly adjusting to the dim light. Shadows stood around me. I brought my hands up, creating a fireball ready for an attack, but one never came. Throughout the room, boxes stood three high.

"Sure are jumpy tonight," Grace stated, then sang, "Jump, dance, let's make sweet love tonight."

"What song is that?" I asked, moving through the maze.

I flipped the light switch, and they flickered on. My room had been erased. The bed frame leaned against one wall while my little glowing stars that had been on my ceiling were lying in a pile on the floor. Painting supplies were spread out on a white tarp against one freshly painted wall.

He'd packed my life away.

As if I were no longer family.

Don't come home. My heart clenched, and I braced myself on my knees, breathing in and out. *It's okay.* But I couldn't quite squash the feeling that this was our breaking point.

Grace wrapped herself around my bent frame. "I made the song up because I'm getting laid tonight."

I laughed and then smiled. Grace stood as I wiped my face, letting out a long breath.

I pulled her into a hug. "Thank you for being here with me." She didn't say anything but tightened her hold. I let go. "Okay, let's find some clothes."

Opening the closest box, I found my pants neatly folded. I retrieved an extra pair of jeans out of the box and then moved it aside, not bothering to pack it back up. The next one had shirts. I continued until I grabbed enough clothes for a week. The last box had my overnight bag. I started piling in the clothes, but before I could zip it up, Grace held Mr. Rabbit in my face. I took the ragged stuffed animal and squished it into the bag. The room felt more normal now, with the boxes scattered and open, clothes hanging off the sides.

"Now what?" Grace asked.

"I'll leave a note and head back over to the school." I heaved the bag onto my shoulder. "I'm guessing if I ask you to dinner, you'll say you're busy."

She flipped one escaped curl behind her ear. "I love you, but I've had to cancel on my ginger several times now. I'm getting some tonight."

She hugged me again and waved goodbye before light filled the room.

On the way to the stairs, I took notice of my father's untouched office nook. No boxes were stacked high, and all his books, files, and pens sat neatly on his desk. My fingers spasmed at the order of black pens, itching to create a little chaos. My father's other bane. I'd never kept my room showroom ready. It's not that I liked the "chaos," as he would put it, but I didn't really have time to keep it tidy between all my activities. I was just exhausted. Day in and day out. Who wouldn't be with meditation twenty-four seven?

I headed down to leave a note. The rest of the house was exactly the same as the last time I'd been here. The stakes had seemed so high two weeks ago. *Why won't he let me explain what happened?*

I darted my eyes around as I walked into the dining room that connected the kitchen and living room. Nothing was out of place—no moving boxes strewn about or lying against the walls. The living room sat in darkness, but I could see the outline of the couch and rocking chair my father had sat in over the course of my life while he watched his favorite shows.

Sighing, I headed for the magnetic notepad kept on the front of the refrigerator for grocery items. *What should I write to say sorry? Sorry, Dad, for choosing my own path.* But I didn't really feel like I needed to apologize. If we could just have a fucking adult conversation for once, he might understand me.

I jotted down one sentence. *Answer my calls, Dad!* I

ripped that piece off and shoved it into my jeans before writing another, nicer, one. That would have to do for now. *I wish there was a way to show him how I feel.*

My heart constricted as I tightened my hand around the strap of the overnight bag. *How do I get through to him? Where's the unconditional love, Dad?* Growing up in this town with all its prejudices, I hadn't really taken it all to heart. They were people who didn't matter. Dad was my family. This whole situation tore at my soul.

Sighing, I glanced at the dark hallway that housed the picture of my mother and flipped the switch. A small beam of light shot down, giving her frame a halo effect. I stepped closer to look at the contours of her profile. The tattoo on her back seemed more vibrant than normal. I took in the delicate artwork lying diagonally from one shoulder blade to the bottom of her ribs. The bloodstone pommel and darkened leather handle connected to the interlocked double blades, depicting the four elements etched into the steel.

I gasped. It was a replica of her sword, Warrior. No wonder it had been so familiar.

I reached out to touch the frame but stopped short. I missed her so much despite not really knowing her. My powers brought me closer to her, almost as if the aether connected us. I shook my head. My fingers grazed the cold glass. I couldn't take the only picture my father had of my mother. He'd missed her so much.

"Don't worry, Mom. I'll be back." With that goodbye, I turned and headed out the front door.

Two

EMBER

My phone buzzed as I headed to my car. Bob's name came across the screen, reminding me I lost at last night's card game. And I had to buy dinner, yet again. I'd been playing with the demons every night since I moved in. It had helped to distract my mind from the fact that my dad didn't want me.

Luke had played once with us, but he'd mostly stayed in his room since I moved in. He'd shared the first time he met the demons. They'd been sitting in a cobwebbed cafeteria, tossing cards at each other and laughing. Luke barged into the room, hoping to hide from his friends after he'd turned. He hadn't known they were demons when he asked them what they were playing. In unison, one said go fish, while another said poker. Though they had since assured me they mostly played poker, not children's games.

I'd stupidly taught them a new card game called bullshit that I'd learned from Grace. I had been winning most of those games until this week. It was based solely on identifying if the other players were lying. The demons loved it, especially being able to yell bullshit in each other's faces. And of course, they beat me. After losing a week straight, I considered that they were somehow cheating.

The car started as another buzz came through, making the message play through the Bluetooth connection.

"Message received: Bob—Parker Elementary bartender. Mexican," the audio announced.

I replied before pulling out onto the street and heading across town to my favorite Mexican restaurant. At least I could sit and drink a normal margarita—one that didn't get me wasted before I finished it—while I waited and rethought my plan in between delicious sips.

I drove down Main Street past Dad's dark office building. If he wasn't there, and he wasn't at home, *where could he be?* He stopped working late hours years ago when his business grew enough to hire another realtor under him.

It took two trips around Casa del Pecado parking lot before a spot in the back opened. I locked my car and headed to the entrance. Once inside, I squeezed myself into a spot at the bar, ordering the food and my drink.

Several minutes later, the server placed a strawberry margarita in front of me. I sipped slowly, letting the cold drink wash down my throat. *It's not as good as Bob's.*

"Dammit," I whispered into the glass as my chest tightened.

And it's giving me heartburn. I dug through my purse to find a chewable antacid and popped one into my mouth.

What to do about Dad? I needed to get him in person, somewhere he couldn't ignore me. I sighed. But it couldn't be too public. I took another sip, scanning the patrons of the restaurant. The aether caressed my senses with the influx of bodies, bringing in a mixture of visuals. I rarely extended the aether into crowds, but something was causing tension in my shoulders as I sat there drinking.

I tilted my head, looking at a man on the other side of the bar. He faced away from me but had wavy blonde locks similar to Christo's. *Is it him?* I gripped the stem of my glass and waited for the man to turn around. The bartender sat a beer down. *Yes.* Another second and he would turn around. And he did, but it wasn't Chris.

Can I buy you a drink? His silky voice slipped into my mind.

I turned, coming face-to-face with him. *Had I summoned Christo here?* "What are you doing here?"

His smile widened. "Thought you wanted to spend a little time together." He winked and leaned back against the bar, looking relaxed, scanning me from head to toe. "I know I've been busy."

The bond, tying my life to his forever, had alerted him.

I twisted the napkin in my lap. "Stop reading my mind."

He straightened, stepping closer to me as people

moved around us. His breath tickled my ear as he whispered, "I missed you."

I turned to meet his eyes. "I guess I missed you too," I whispered back before he kissed me.

He grinned, leaning against the bar again.

I turned my glass so I could take another drink from the salted rim. "Where did you go last night?"

I'd fallen asleep in his bed only to wake up on the futon at Parker Elementary.

Christo placed his hand on the small of my back as more customers squeezed through the crowd. "You looked so peaceful sleeping. I didn't want to disturb you." He finally sat down on the newly opened stool, moving my legs in between his. He laid his hands on my knees. "I had a job to take care of."

"So not Elder business?"

He shook his head, his blonde locks sweeping in front of his eyes. "No, a contract."

I took another long sip, eyeing the half-empty glass. He refused to talk about his contract work with me, so I knew not to bother.

"When's your next task for the Elders?"

He hadn't really shared that much about what he was required to do.

The bartender sat a piña colada down in front of Chris.

He flicked the umbrella out of the glass before taking a drink. "How do you like these?"

I laughed. "I usually go for the margaritas. Not much of a coconut person."

He smiled, reaching for my glass. "Let me try this, then."

"No." I pulled my glass out of range, sloshing it over the edge. "Oops." Giggling, I sat my glass on the bar, looking for napkins, but the only ones were on the other side of Christo. *What's wrong with me?* I held out my hand. "Can you pass those?"

He took my hand, bringing it to his lips, licking the margarita mixture off my fingers. I let him do it before regaining my senses and pulling away. I peeked around curiously, but no one seemed to care. They were all too busy with their own lives. I sneaked a look back at Christo. *God, he was sexy.*

I gulped down the lump in my throat. "So, the Elders?"

He sat up a little straighter. "Tonight, but I don't know what it is yet." He took another long pull of his frozen, fruity drink. His face scrunched up, and he set it aside. He lifted his hand, and the bartender returned, despite the crowd. Chris ordered a beer and turned back to me. "I doubt I can come see you tonight."

"I understand." I stuck my bottom lip out, pretending to pout.

The server brought two to-go bags to the counter.

"Are you hungry?"

"I'm taking dinner back to Parker Elementary for everyone."

The server came back with the receipt. I thanked them and grabbed one of the bags. Chris took the other.

He wrapped his arm around my shoulder, and we made our way through the busy restaurant.

"Why didn't you invite me?" he asked as we walked out toward my car.

"I didn't know what your plans were, and honestly, you aren't on speaking terms with my friends," I said, glancing at him. "They think you abandoned us at Rabon's."

His expression didn't change as we made our way through the parked cars, but his fingers across my back tensed before he released me.

I set my bag on the hood of my car and unlocked the door.

"You could introduce me as your boyfriend. Maybe that would resolve the situation."

I cringed at the thought. *No, not yet.* I wasn't ready to tell my friends about the bonding. The ritual had been completed without my consent, to save my life. There were too many uncertainties. If I was the Zodian Warrior, would Rabon try to attack us again?

"I will," I started, and he handed me the takeout. "But not right now."

"I want your happiness, but sooner rather than later, you're going to tell your friends about me," he warned, backing into the shadows.

"Wait."

But as he reemerged from the darkness, my breath caught. His beauty never stopped mesmerizing me. His hair came down around his eyes. I itched to brush my fingers through those curls.

"Yes?" he questioned.

Do I ask him? Would he know or even answer, unlike Lyra?

"Ask, Ember," he said.

I gulped down the tightness in my throat. "Am I the Zodian Warrior?"

His eyebrows rose. "Yes." He placed his hand over my bracelet. "It's why your mark differs from the two other Zodians."

My body released much of the tension I'd been holding at his words. Warmth spread through me at finally having someone give me a straight answer. *No more secrets.*

"So Rabon is after me?"

"You won't have to worry about that after the gala."

"Gala?" I questioned.

"It's the end of my trials, and after my ascension, you'll have the entire Immortal Society at your call." He stepped forward and kissed the top of my head. "It's in three months. You'll need a gown." He paused, rubbing the back of his neck. "And you're going to have to meet my mother."

The aether stirred, letting me know he'd vanished. An Immortal gala. Or meeting his mother. *I didn't know which sounded worse.*

<hr>

"What took ya so long?" Bob asked as I entered the cafeteria.

He took one bag from me and proceeded to the table where the others sat. Over the last two weeks, I had gotten to meet Bob's closest friends, Chase and Scout. The three were an interesting trio. The aether always brought back Golden Girls when they were around, and they argued like old ladies too. Neither liked people very much. The first day I moved in, they avoided me, but once I asked to join their card game, they started chatting like we'd been friends for years.

Luke materialized beside me, and a chill swept down my arms. He took the other bag and passed the to-go boxes around the eight-person table. But I couldn't shake the sensation the aether had brought me.

"Luke," I started.

He smiled in my direction—the same way that made him my Luke all those years ago before Dad forced us apart. "You had the chicken and rice?"

I nodded, taking the container from him.

"You want a drink?" Bob asked from behind the bar. "I've created a new recipe I'm calling Bloody Hex."

Scout shouted, "I helped with the name!"

"Nah, I drank one at the restaurant while I waited."

"Was it that busy?" Scout asked, shoveling in food between his words.

I grimaced at the rice spilling over the table onto the floor. "Very busy," I said, leaving out the time I'd spent with Christo. "Honestly, I didn't realize you guys ate so much human food. You've consumed more than growing teenage boys since I've been here."

Bob sat down across from me but said nothing before digging into his food.

Scout coughed. "We eat all kinds of things, but mostly human food. We"—Scout gestured to himself and the other two demons—"are herbivores."

"Meaning we don't eat humans or drink their blood." Chase smirked at Luke.

Luke paused, the fork halfway to his mouth, before his eyes landed on Chase. It seemed like they darkened. I tensed, but then he blinked, and they were normal. He continued chowing down on his food without commenting.

I turned back to the ladies trio. Chase and Scout could pass for human, except for their pointed ears and unnatural reddish skin, and I wondered if they were half human. Bob, on the other hand, was more demon-y than the others. His horns poked through his long, curly dark hair.

"You two are half human?" I asked, after washing down my food with water.

They nodded while Chase spoke. "We have just enough of Brelgarun in our appearance that makes most humans shy away. We can, on occasion, go out into the human world. Movie theaters are easy to go unnoticed."

I turned to Bob. "What kind of demon are you?"

"What does it matter?" he asked between bites. "Regthod."

I shrugged. "It doesn't, just curious about your cultures and why you three are hiding out in Happy Valley."

I picked up my fork, and all three demons turned their attention to me.

"Who said we were hiding out?" Chase sputtered.

Bob sighed, and I smirked. Luke's eyes widened at the intel. I'd been living here for two weeks, and while the demon bar was open to any demons, the only ones who came through the cafeteria door were traveling in the area and didn't stay long. Mostly to wait out the daylight to travel in darkness. Bob and his two so-called friends had been here longer than Luke had been a vampire. They had taken shelter when the building had been listed as condemned.

Scout hit Chase in the chest. "She knows now."

"I didn't really until Bob sighed." I smiled at him. "So, why are you guys in hiding?"

Bob spoke for the three. "Most demons live in a community of their species, but us three misfits didn't get along with the rest of them and were banished." He paused, taking a bite without chewing. "Most who don't have a community join Rabon's elite army or die."

Luke tensed, and I reached my hand under the table to rest it on top of his. Squeezing, he gave me a slight nod before he relaxed. Two weeks ago, we fought against Rabon to save lives, and while we won their freedom, it hadn't been easy. We had lost Nathan. The memorial a few days ago had been a somber event.

"Done?" Luke asked, picking up my empty carton.

I nodded, and he proceeded out the door back to his room. The aether followed him until his door shut behind him. He'd taken Nathan's death the hardest, and none of us knew how to reach him. He seemed to spiral more and more each day.

"What's gotten into him?" Scout asked. "He never plays cards anymore."

"You in, Ember?" Chase asked, shuffling the deck.

I nodded. "One round. So why did you not want to join Rabon?"

All three paused what they were doing.

"Are you kidding?" Bob asked from his seat. "He's a monster who wants to take over the world and dominate the weak."

"You met him," Chase uttered at the same time Scout hissed, "Never."

"Okay, just making sure you're on our side when he shows up to kill me," I said.

"He's a tyrant who's wiped out several races, including most of yours. It would be smart of you to stay clear of him like we have done," Bob stated.

I nodded. "Let's play," I chimed, easing the tension in the room.

Three

LUKE

Laughter floated through the closed door; Ember had agreed to play cards again tonight. The three amigos hadn't been this lively in a long time. I should have been happy, but it was so fucking annoying. This place used to be my sanctuary. *Now she's here all the time.* And I didn't know how to tell her what Rabon kept claiming. Hell, I didn't know what to do about it myself.

Losing Nathan shattered Ted. He'd tried to hide it from everyone, but I knew he was hurting. *I'm part of that reason.* I pushed forward and slammed my fist into the bathroom door, pushing it open. Turning the water on, I waited for the room to steam up before undressing and climbing under the pellets of hot water.

Why did I have to get her involved? How can I stop all of this?

The shower was supposed to calm me down, but the drops of water abraded my skin. The scalding water turned cold. I turned the knobs off and left the shower.

After stumbling across the room, I leaned against the sink, staring at my reflection. I gripped the porcelain, and it chipped under my will. I sighed at the pleasure in that tiny destruction. *Shit.* I scrubbed my fingers through my hair, flinging water droplets before wiping them off my face.

I left the bathroom and sat on my bed. Ted had left papers on the coffee table with information about the Chaos Brothers. *I don't want to face the reality of my research.* I flung the table halfway across the room. All of its contents scattered and shattered on the concrete floor. A silence descended in the room. A sigh escaped my lips once more.

Laughter came from down the hall. *Fuck.*

I grabbed some clothes and headed to the gym. I processed better when I was pounding at the bag. Connecting my phone to the overhead speaker, I blared my workout music.

I wrapped my hands before putting on my gloves. After steadying the bag and testing the gloves, I fired off several combos.

I am not Istros.

It made no sense. Why was my body warm? Why didn't I crave blood like all the other vampires? I'd been different from the very beginning.

The only way to get past this was to find out the truth.

It didn't taken long to build up a sweat. I jumped up and down for a few seconds, shaking my body loose after the workout. *I need more information.*

Four

EMBER

I groaned, climbing out of the futon. *Why are they so uncomfortable?* I cursed myself for playing cards late into the night. *At least I didn't lose again.*

Stretching, I watched the retractable shutters close over the windows for the day. Luke had spent a small fortune to fix the condemned school after his family had purchased it. Parker Elementary had housed grades three through five, and it was where Grace and I had become best friends. I was educated here for two years before it had closed.

The townspeople rumored that Luke Bowen was part of a special military ops team headquartered in Happy Valley. I smiled. If only they knew what he really was, they would flee in a heartbeat or bring the pitchforks.

I'd taken the nurse's office on the first floor because of the attached bathroom. The first level had an admin office, library, gym, and a few classrooms. Luke slept in the basement that housed the cafeteria and smaller classrooms.

The pain in my back subsided as I moved around the room working my muscles. I stopped in front of the bag I'd thrown on the floor yesterday. My clothes had spilled out onto the tile. Work was in three hours, and I'd scheduled another training session with Lyra. I needed to remember to bring a change of clothes. I crouched down by the pile, sifting through the layers before my eyes shifted to the coffee table.

My mother's box sat on top of the cherry wood. Mocking me. It had no visible seams. Nothing showed how, or even if, it opened. Only a deep feeling within told me I would find answers inside.

The wooden box wasn't huge. Twelve inches wide and seven inches long with about another seven inches in height with steel corners. Lines carved into the box met at the top, forming a symbol I knew well. My left hand reached toward my right wrist where my dark tawny leather wrap lay. People hardly noticed it since it blended into my skin tone. Dad had gifted it to me when I was six years old, stating that it belonged to my mother and telling me to keep my birthmark hidden. It made sense, now that I knew Rabon was after me.

Hesitantly, I stared at the bracelet and the identical markings. "How do you open?"

I lifted the box and shook it. Nothing rattled inside. I raised it high above my head before slamming my arms down, releasing the box. It crashed against the floor and rolled back under the side table. Click.

The small sound gave me hope it opened, but as I pulled it back out, it was unscathed. I tossed it back onto the bed. *Damn, nothing has worked so far.*

"Ember." My name was followed by a hard knock. "Ember," Luke shouted through the door.

"One sec." I set the box in my suitcase and closed the lid on top of it, letting the clothes hide it from view.

Outside my door, Luke stood dressed in workout clothes. "Meet me in the gym." He turned, calling over his shoulder, "Bring the sword."

Tempted to salute his backside, I shook my head as I closed the door. After finding a clean pair of workout clothes, I tied my hair in a bun at my nape. I grabbed Warrior, my mother's sword.

Luke was stretching when I walked in. He gestured toward the mat, and I trotted forward, placing the weapon out of the way. I mimicked his moves. Ten minutes later, warm-ups were completed, and he picked up Warrior and unsheathed it. He touched the blade and winced.

"I figured I didn't need to tell you it's sharp," I said at the sight of his blood dripping onto the mat.

He licked the wound and handed the sword back to me. "Did you sharpen it recently?"

I admired the elements etched on the steel blade. The sleek bloodstone grip fit perfectly in my hand. The edge of the blade glinted in the fluorescent lights.

"No, it's been in storage for twenty years."

"Hm, maybe it's always magically sharp."

I didn't really know. I was hoping that and so many

more secrets would be in Mom's box, and I could learn about them. If I could just open it.

"You might be right. Where do you want to start today?" I held it out in front of me.

He'd been helping me work on my swordsmanship since I moved in and showed him my weapon.

"Balancing," he said as he reached to push my arms into the right position.

Luke stepped over to the wall where his collection of assorted weapons hung. He grabbed a broadsword, coming to stand a few feet from me where I could still see what he was doing.

"On the count of three." He counted, then he moved forward with his right foot. As he brought his left foot to match the other, he sliced downward, diagonally, with his sword.

I followed his movements. We made circles around the mat until my arms were aching. Luke counted the steps out loud.

"Are you teaching me dance steps?" I asked.

He chuckled. "It has the same rhythm."

We made a few more rounds before Luke stopped to look at me. "I think you're ready for a match."

I shifted, relaxing my arm that held Warrior to glance at him. "Really?"

"Why not? It's not like you can kill me."

We squared. I tightened my hands around the grip. He disappeared. Using the aether to guide me, I brought the blade up on my right side to block. His eyes widened as our swords clanged. He spun backward, putting some distance between us.

The fluorescent lights illuminated the heavy practice mat where I stood poised at the ready.

With the hum of artificial lights in the background, he said, "That was good, but make sure you are centered. If I pushed a little bit more, you would have toppled over."

I nodded, and he charged me head-on.

The clang of metal echoed off the walls—a crescendo to our dance. Luke provided feedback, helping me navigate the intricacies of our combat within the confines of the gym.

With each exchange, I grew more confident, my movements becoming more fluid and controlled.

He jumped back, landing halfway on the mat. I sprinted forward, seeing his balance teetering, but he was ready. He connected with my blade perfectly to send it flying out of my hands.

With his arm extended, I was able to bring my right hook straight to his chin, adding a little bit of flame to distract him. He pulled back, and I dashed toward Warrior. Once it was in my hands again, he gave me a sly grin.

"Neat trick." He rubbed his chin. "You should do that more, but don't lose your sword next time."

But I couldn't help thinking maybe if I'd brought Warrior with us . . . "Nathan might still be . . ." I stopped. There were so many variables that night.

"Ember," Luke shouted from the other side of the room.

When I locked eyes with him, I blurted, "You know if Christo could have gotten back in . . ."

He gritted his teeth before answering. "None of that was your fault. Rabon is to blame."

Silence followed that statement. I didn't know what to say. It somehow felt like my fault. I was the only one on the balcony with Nathan. If he hadn't tried to save me . . .

I wiped my eyes with my forearm. "All right, let's finish this."

The space around us transformed into a battleground once again with the energy fueling our practice as we honed our skills together.

He rushed me straight on, and the fluorescent light caught his irises. For an instant, they appeared blood red. I faltered a step back, landing on the side of my foot. His sword sliced downward. I brought Warrior in front of me to block, but his strength pushed me to my knees. I held my breath as he pressed down on me. *He won. Why isn't he stopping?*

"Luke," I yelled.

My arm trembled, but he refused to relent. I locked onto his eyes. They held no emotion. *Is he actually trying to kill me?* Instinct kicked in, and my flames surrounded me.

He jumped back, landing in a crouch, his face buried in his knees.

I collapsed on the mat, panting as I eyed him. "What the hell was that?" I hissed through deep breaths.

He let out a long breath before making eye contact. "Testing you."

"Testing me. Are you kidding me?" I marched over to him. "What's going on with you?"

He stood. "You need to mix your sword and fire together."

I gaped at him. "I know but—" I didn't finish before he disappeared through the door.

What the hell? His eyes were red like they had been last night at dinner. I knew I needed to work more on using both of the skills together, but it wasn't like him at all. He'd always been a teacher at heart. He trained elementary school students in boxing at the local Y. It melted my heart to see him bend down to the kids' level to listen patiently to their questions that had nothing to do with the sport.

I sat cross-legged on the dust-covered concrete, looking out at the range's target area. I'd worked two hours earlier to cover Hannah's empty position. After being rescued, Hannah had wasted no time in proposing to Doug. They'd said goodbye to Happy Valley to travel the world. It sucked that I had just renewed my friendship with her and she decided to leave, but I wished her the best. I cried the day she left. It would be sad to not see her smiling face every day or to gossip during down times at work. Those spare moments with her made me forget my anger at Dad's denial. And the loss of Nathan. I wiped the wetness from my eyes as my phone beeped.

"Hey," I said to Lyra.

"Are you crying?" she asked as I sniveled into the phone.

"I'm fine."

"You don't sound okay, kid."

"Are you ready to train?" I asked, climbing to my feet.

There wasn't a reason to get into a discussion with her about Dad. She'd never seemed to get it. Like she was void of all emotions most days. There had been a handful of times I'd seen her not be calm and collected, but when it came to my dad, she couldn't care less.

"What's bothering you?" she said. "Let's get that out of the way first."

I huffed. It was pointless to tell her, but by the sound of her voice, I knew she wouldn't drop it until I did. "I stopped by Dad's."

"And did he give you trouble?"

"He wasn't there, but he packed my entire room into boxes." My pulse quickened at the picture of boxes being stacked neatly in an unrecognizable room. *Did she hear me?*

"That's rough, buddy."

I rolled my eyes. "Thanks."

"Don't roll your eyes at me."

She always seemed to know. "Give better advice." *Or at least care a little*. But I didn't really mean it.

I knew she cared about me. It was Dad that she

wanted to cut out of my life. *She just may get what she wants.*

She sneered, "My advice is that you don't need him in your life. You don't need anyone in your life. They just let you down when you need them. But I didn't really think you wanted to hear that now."

She was right. I didn't want to hear it. I had to believe Dad would come around. He would have to. I just needed to catch him at home and explain my side to him. He loved me. Talking to him face-to-face would help. Staying calm and not getting upset during the conversation would also help.

"If you're not ready for training—"

I cut her off. "No, I need to do more."

"Remember not to get too burned out. Practice is good, but if you're dead tired, then you'll get nowhere." She paused. "You've been practicing with the sword."

"Yes, I remember what you said."

I'd told Lyra about the sword a few days earlier. She'd seemed surprised and curious to know how Dad had come by it. And from my descriptions, she was sure it was a legit family heirloom. One created by the thirteenth original ruling tribe.

"That sword is a part of you. An extension of your body. Once you've perfected your form, you'll be able to channel the elements through the sword, which will amplify their power. But for now, let's see if you can travel using Agni."

"What?" I sputtered, not recognizing the term.

"Remember how you teleported from Canada to Happy Valley?"

"Of course." I'd traveled through the lightning, and I was pretty sure that's how Luke and I ended up in the school gym instead of the bottom of the ocean.

"Agni is traveling through the lightning, and is the last form fire takes. Once you learn to use Agni, you'll be a master of flames. Then we will move on to the other elements."

It seemed far-fetched that I would have mastered my fire, but I had improved quickly since coming home. Something had clicked into place after almost losing Ted. Setting him on fire without hurting him opened my eyes to what I could really do. And I was more than ready to start learning about the other elements.

"This power is very dangerous if done wrong, but it can be an excellent tool in battle." Lyra continued, "You also need to make sure your energy level is high. You need to be hyperfocused on where you are traveling to."

"All right."

"The more rested you are, the stronger your powers will be, and it will determine how far you can travel using Agni. Take a stance. Concentrate on drawing the surrounding aether into your body and then slowly releasing it back into the universe, but let the energy take you with it." Her voice came through crackly, and I glanced at the screen to see if the connection had dropped. "Well, are you doing it?"

"One moment."

"Take all the time you need."

I rolled my eyes again, and she sighed through the phone. Ignoring her, I stood in the sandy grass at the edge of the target area with my feet braced apart, hands down at my sides. I pulled the energy from around me like I was creating a fireball. When the energy built up, a hum surrounded me, the rocks at my feet vibrating. I took a deep breath in, confused at the pool-like scent in the air, and with my exhale, I let the buildup release, projecting myself to the other side of the range.

Lightning rained down upon me. I dodged it, hitting the dirt before the sky cleared.

"I'm guessing that's a no."

I climbed to my feet, wiping the loose sand off my pants. "Correct," I said. "I'll try again."

"You do that, kid. I have to run. Talk to you in a few days."

The line clicked dead before I could say anything. Typical for my set of friends. Between Lyra and Grace, I didn't know who left me hanging more. Kaity hadn't yet, but I wasn't sure if she considered me a friend. As an ancestral witch, she seemed to be the most knowledgeable around here. Kaity might be able to help me learn this power. I knew respectfully that our powers weren't the same, but since she could create fireballs, it wasn't a bad idea to ask. Since Lyra hadn't given me much to go on.

Five

EMBER

I gritted my teeth against the phone pressed to my ear. "Dad, we need to talk, please. Let me tell you my side." I pressed the end call button and rounded the corner, heading for the cafeteria.

Shouts came from the open doorway, but I already knew what was going on. Chris's aetheric signature had landed in the school a few minutes earlier, and it was clear from the gang's mumblings that they didn't think too highly of him. I didn't know *why* he was here, though.

My eyes found him the moment I stepped foot into the room. *God, why does he have to be so magnetic?* He was leaning against a table, his head cocked in my direction, a small smile playing on his lips.

I walked farther into the room where Ted and Luke were yelling. Kaity and Grace sat calmly at one of the tables, waiting. There was no sign of Bob or the half demons. They avoided confrontation like the plague.

Christo's smile grew when I walked straight toward him.

Jerking, I moved around him to sit beside Grace and Kaity. "What's going on?" I asked.

Luke answered, "He thinks we're going to let him join us."

I pivoted to look at Chris. What was he planning? We spent the early morning together, and he, yet again, never mentioned he would be here for today's meeting—the first after Nathan's death. He had never bothered to come to any others.

Christo stepped closer. "I'm here to offer my services." He smirked. "I can be quite good in a fight."

"Maybe if you stuck around," Ted uttered.

Christo shrugged. "I left to get the vampires off me. But they blocked me from reentry."

"We don't need your help," Ted spat, his fists clenched at his sides.

Chris held his palms in the air. "I only offer because of the mess at Rabon's."

"What are you talking about?" asked Kaity.

"You guys are lucky you escaped his clutches. And well, he doesn't like to lose," Chris said. "He'll retaliate if you don't watch your asses."

My eyes met Luke's copper ones, and I knew he was remembering those few seconds before he jumped over the balcony rail, risking sun exposure to save me. He hadn't known I could use my powers to transport us to the safety of the school. I hadn't even known I would either.

"You can't stay!" Ted shouted, bringing my attention back to the cafeteria.

"Why not?" I blurted out, unable to stop myself. All eyes turned to me. "We could use the help. There are only four of us now that Nathan is gone." I paused, clearing my throat.

Ted took a step closer. "What the hell, Ember? You and Luke almost died, too, because he couldn't follow directions."

"Another person could be helpful," Kaity squeaked.

"We can't all be out every night. We need more breaks." My eyes landed back on Chris.

He regarded Luke, knowing his word was final. Luke had started the group after he turned into a vampire, and the others had followed him.

Luke nodded. "Fine." He turned toward me. "But you're on babysitting duty."

The others grumbled but gathered at the table to begin while Christo stood in the background. We'd been meeting once a week for a few months to go over patrol schedules. I shifted my glance to Christo. He stood tall despite not being invited to sit with us. As we came to the end of the meeting, they started discussing the weekend patrols.

Using our ability to speak mind-to-mind, I asked him, *What are you up to?*

His eyes landed on mine, and he smiled. *I want to spend more time with you.*

You didn't need to join the team.

Ah, but I did. Maybe if I'm here more often, you'll tell our friends about us sooner rather than later.

That was what Christo wanted. *Does he even care what I want?* I bit my lip. I just needed time to get used to all of this. It wasn't like I could hide a secret boyfriend forever. His eyes twinkled at me—letting me know, once again, that he knew what I was thinking.

I frowned. That was never going to get easier.

I turned back to the group to find they were still talking about the weekend plans. In an effort to distract myself from the hunk standing on the other side of the room, I visualized the lesson from earlier today in my head. It hadn't really been that productive. What if the reason I couldn't use Agni correctly was that I hadn't been at full strength? I had stayed out another hour working on it, but the energy seemed off from the time I used it to flee Christo.

The others stood as one and realized Christo was still there. They started pairing off, but the arguing about him joining the team started again.

"Enough," I yelled. "I really just want to get out there and get back so I can sleep."

"You're grumpy," Ted chided as he walked out with Kaity, who crinkled her eyes.

Grace nodded her agreement before disappearing in a ball of her light.

"Lucky me," Chris said, heading for the door. "I'm going with you guys."

I raked my gaze over Luke's—he hadn't moved—and I shrugged it off. Chris coming with the two of us was probably the safest route. I could be there to listen to the conversation and reroute it if anything about *us* was mentioned. Behind me, the familiar scent of chalk dust engulfed me, reminding me of the times I hung out with Luke at the gym. He walked beside me.

The three of us piled into my car. Luke leaned toward the passenger side window in the front next to me, and Chris sat behind him. I turned the ignition on and headed out of the parking lot.

"Move up," Christo ordered from the back seat.

Luke turned slightly but kept silent as he leaned the seat farther back.

"Hey!" Christo yelled.

I slammed on the brakes. "Chris, just sit behind me," I hissed as the two stared daggers at each other.

He slid over, and his knees pushed against the back of my seat. Again, I started in the direction of our assigned area for tonight—the southwest subdivision. The town blurred past, and I tried to avoid meeting Chris's gaze in the rearview mirror. Finally, I parked at the old church Dad used to bring me to before I headed to college. I shut the car off, and we got out.

Christo climbed out of the car. "When was this church abandoned?"

"I don't know," I said, unable to tear my gaze away from the dilapidated building. "I haven't really been to church in a while."

If someone renovated it and removed the cross that stood at the entrance, it would blend in with the other houses in the area. One of the double doors was slightly ajar, flapping with the whipping wind from the north. There were several broken windows, and papers were scattered across the lawn, dancing on the breeze as if they had a mind of their own.

"There's someone inside," Luke said, nodding to Chris.

Chris nodded back, and the two of them went into the church as if they had run operations together before.

I shook my head. *Men.*

I went to the trunk to grab my mother's sword. While I was more comfortable with a bow in my hand, it lay there broken from my tumble with Kit. I hadn't seen him since that night at the range and had no idea why he'd attacked me. But I couldn't buy a new one on my part-time salary. I was proving that I could be better with the sword when I used my abilities as well.

The aether slithered around me. Chills raced up my arms in warning, but when I turned, there was just a teenager standing in the barren parking lot. I glanced around but didn't see anyone else. I took a step toward the young girl. Her skin was unusually pale, and I guessed she might be around sixteen.

"Are you okay?" I asked.

"They attacked me," she started. "I want to go home, b-but I can't go inside."

She tensed when she seemed to spot the sword in my hand.

"It's okay. I can help you get home," I said, slowly lowering the weapon to my side. "Who attacked you?"

"I don't know. Some old man." She started crying. Between broken breaths she begged, "Please help me."

"I will. Don't worry."

She was only inches away now. Her neck bore two puncture holes. *A vampire attack.*

I pivoted, bringing my arm up to block, only to slide back on the gravel, the aether's warning too late. I lost my grip on the sword. It sang as it flew through the air, landing close to the young girl's feet.

"She's such a good little pet," the vampire said, his mouth covered in blood. "You smell delicious."

"She's mine," another voice said, emerging from the shadows.

I anchored myself as I eyed the four new vampires at the edge of the parking lot. They were pale and gaunt, staring at me. Eyes bloodshot. One licked his lips, running his tongue along his fang.

I shuddered at the action. I glanced back at the church doors Luke and Christo had vanished through. Hopefully, they would hear the commotion out here and return. *Unless they ran into more vampires inside.*

He pounced, and I rolled away, reaching for Warrior. My fingers grazed the hilt, but he dragged me backward along the rough gravel.

"Please help me," the girl shrieked, standing a few feet from us.

I kicked at the vampire, gaining enough room to stand. I threw a right hook engulfed in flames that connected with his face, my knuckles gleaming with blood from the impact.

"Help me!"

I couldn't stop myself from looking at the girl, even though I knew it was a trap. She was standing there, her hands clasped to her heart. *Is there a way to help her? Had he turned her yet?*

The vampire grabbed my throat, nails digging into my skin. I locked eyes with him and smirked. I unleashed the fire inside me, engulfing his entire body in flames. A second later, he was ash, and the others fled into the night.

A high-pitched scream shattered the night.

I spun around. Her eyes locked with mine a split second before Luke sliced through her neck with Warrior. The terrified teenager's mouth hung open as her head tumbled to the ground, and her scream went silent forever. Chills ran down my spine. Luke's demeanor was calm, but the moonlight revealed a hint of ruby gleaming in his irises.

I screamed.

"What's wrong?" Chris asked, appearing at my side. He grabbed my face, making me look him in the eyes, and he checked to make sure I wasn't injured. "Ember, what's wrong?"

Tears pooled in my eyes. "I told her I would help her," I said, my voice barely a whisper. And then louder, I asked, "Why did you kill her?" I pointed at Luke, who had moved closer when Chris had touched my face.

His eyebrow rose, but he stayed silent.

I brushed off Christo's arm and stormed over to Luke,

poking him in the chest. He released the sword, and it clanked to the ground.

"She needed our help. Not death!" I rose to my tiptoes, jabbing my finger hard into his chest. He grabbed my upper arms, pulling me closer. "How could you?" I shouted, flinging my arms up and smacking him in the jaw.

Luke let go of me.

Christo's arms encircled me from behind, pulling me from Luke's grasp. He hugged me into his chest. His heart beat wildly in my ear.

He leaned down and whispered, "Be still."

I let loose a breath as the rhythm of his heart slowed.

He tightened his arms around me, enveloping me with his warmth. "She was a vampire, Em. There wasn't anything we could have done."

I sputtered, "She asked for help. I promised her I would help. Maybe we could have turned her back."

"There's no coming back from death." Luke's bitter words turned sour in my mouth.

I'd let the teenage girl down.

Seconds later, a phone rang, and Christo released me, and his solid presence moved away to answer the call.

"Let's call it quits for tonight," Luke said, steering me back toward my car.

I shrugged off his hands and stepped away.

He backed off, eyes wide. Then he disappeared.

"Luke," I started but didn't know what to say.

I waited for Christo to return and then retrieved Warrior.

"Are you sure you're okay?" he asked, glancing around. "Where did vampire boy go?"

"He left."

Christo's face softened. "Ember, there wasn't anything you could have done for that girl." He wiped the tears from my cheeks.

I didn't say anything and stepped back. Chris's body tensed, and I turned away, climbing into the driver's seat. Chris remained standing outside. I started the car and rolled down the window.

"I have another meeting." He leaned inside, kissing my head before he, too, disappeared.

I put the car in gear and sped out of the parking lot, heading back to the school. *What has gotten into Luke?* He had always been so patient, looking for the best possible solutions, and he always listened. He cared about what people were feeling. I parked crooked, rushed inside, and sprinted down the hallway to his room. I burst through, not bothering to knock.

Even in the darkness, the aether conveyed emptiness. I knew no one was there. I created a fireball to find the light switch.

"What the hell?"

Trash, papers, and glass were scattered across the floor. The coffee table was upside down.

"Luke, what's going on?" I muttered to myself.

Six

LUKE

I crouched low in the tree's darkness, scanning the park. *What is it about this place?*

I caught the scent of the five vampires who had fled and followed it through the streets to the deserted park. They stood in a semicircle around the entrance, laughing about the recruit dying on her first day—the girl I killed. *Assholes.* Ember's tear-streaked face as she fled my arms flashed before me. The fuckers chuckled into the night, and my fists clenched.

I stepped out of the shadows, taking even strides in their direction. It took them too long to notice me. I grabbed the closest vampire and held him off the ground, digging my nails into his neck. Blood exploded from his veins. *Fuck.* The vamps would have had to drink a victim's blood in the last several hours for him to be bleeding out. He could only hiss as he tried to claw my hand off him.

The vampire farthest from me, wearing a leather

jacket, asked, "What do you want, boy?" Tattoos cascaded down his neck, disappearing below his shirt.

I turned to him. "You're going to tell me where the other vampire nests are located."

He huffed. "And if we don't, you're gonna kill us?"

My smile widened. "I'm killing you eith—"

The leader launched at me, his hands outstretched like cat claws. His friend beside him unsheathed a curved knife and darted toward my side.

I squeezed hard, relieving the vermin of its head; dust flew into the air.

Centering my body, I stepped with my right foot, kicking my left leg up to connect with the leader, sending him flying back toward the broken gate.

Gaining momentum from the kick, I turned to the man holding the knife and knocked his wrist to the side. The blade sliced through my shirt, cutting into my bicep. Blood spilled from the wound. The vampire became hyper focused on the wrong lure. He pushed deeper with his knife, making more droplets of temptation. His tongue extended, eyes wide. I grabbed his arm and twisted it. The blade slipped from his grasp. He thrust his fangs toward my wound. I pivoted my shoulders, bringing my hand down on his back, and kneed him in the face. He sank to the ground. I flipped the knife and stabbed it directly into his heart.

The air shifted when I reached for my stake. The remaining guy, who was standing back to observe, began to flee. *Fucking coward.* I tossed the stake in the air. It flipped twice before I caught it. I hurled it through the night air at my target. The thud carried through the park. And dust floated down to the dewy grass.

"Motherfucker."

I turned to the low, raspy voice at my feet. Grabbing his dirty hair, I bent down to retrieve the curved knife from his heart. I jerked it out of him before pulling on his head, extending it long enough to slice through his throat. I dug deep, pulling at his head with each slice. Finally, the last thread tore from his body. Sour blood splattered onto the ground. I grinned at the thud of the body hitting the ground at my feet and its head as my prize. An instant later, the vampire dematerialized to dust.

The smallest of the vampires stood still, his hands up. "I don't have any beef with you, man."

I cackled, my palm smacking the guy hard across his nose. He flew a couple of feet before crashing down on the ground, his arms spread wide like he was about to make a snow angel. I slipped out my extra stake.

"Pests bother me," I hissed, throwing the wooden stake into his heart. Ash replaced his body. "It does look like an angel," I muttered.

One to go. I brushed the specks of decay off, slowly approaching their leader. Earlier, my kick had sent him flying against the broken gate, and two of the wood poles had pierced his body. Good for me, they were below his heart. He could still very much tell me what I needed to know.

I'll make him pay for what he did to that girl and Ember.

The leader grunted as he tried to heave himself off the broken posts.

"Now you'll have to answer my question."

"What are you?" he asked, eyeing my fangs and the blood dripping from my bicep.

I stepped closer, my face inches from his. "A monster," I whispered. I grabbed his right arm, straightening it out from his body, and placed my foot on the iron. "Where are the nests?"

"I don't know what you're talking about."

I severed his arm from his body. "Wrong answer," I hissed.

He screamed, thrashing against the restraints.

"Now, would you like to keep the other arm?"

The vampire grunted, his body shaking as if he was trying to catch his breath. "I . . ." He uttered between deep heaves. "We left. Started our own. They moved on."

I pulled his other arm tight, the leather ripped with each leisurely tug. "Not good enough."

The vampire's cries rent the sky.

I loosened my grasp on his arm, giving him a small respite. With one last yank, bones and tendons broke free, and I sighed with pleasure at the sound. I held the arm, bringing it close to my face.

"Nice leathers," I said before it crumbled to ash.

I stepped back, eyeing my handy work. A smile spread across my face, and a light breeze brought the scent of burnt forest to my nose—the same one that seemed to cling to Ember. *What is his play?*

"You weren't invited," I said, not bothering to turn around.

"I see we had the same idea," Christo said.

I turned to glare at the demon who thought he was one of us. "I take care of my own."

The demon's body clenched at my words. *Interesting. What does he want with Ember?*

"Did *he* tell you what you wanted?"

I turned back to the vampire; he seemed to be in a trance of some kind. I grasped one of the two poles embedded in him, yanking it through his stomach before stabbing him in the heart with it. Ashes spread on the wind, and I tossed the splintered wood aside.

"So?"

"No," I said, an idea forming in my mind. "Why don't you get me what I need? Call it your ticket to being part of the team."

He narrowed his eyes at my suggestion.

"Or don't bother coming back." *What other reason would he be hanging around?*

Chris sighed. "I don't know why you guys won't believe that I'm here to help." He stood silent for a minute.

I turned to head home. I'd gotten what I needed for now. I'd fed my rage.

"What is it you need?"

Seven

LUKE

I leaned against the solid oak door, breathing in deeply and wishing the smell of death would disappear. My fist clenched as I relived the incident in the park once more. A clean stake to the heart would have been enough. *Why did I take it so far?* I closed my eyes. *It doesn't make sense.*

When I opened them again, my vision blurred red. Nausea danced at the top of my stomach, a sensation I hadn't had since I was a child riding my first roller coaster. The discomfort subsided, and a white-covered field came into view with withered corn stalks sticking through the snow. I reached out to one, and my fingers brushed against the hard and brittle husk. The stalks disintegrated at the mere touch. *What the fuck?*

I pulled back, watching blood drip from my fingertips onto the ground, puddling like ink blotches in the snow, but when I ventured back to where the corn stalks once were, a man stood there instead. A deep gash was cut across his throat, and a look of terror marred his face. I stepped away from the corpse but tripped over something and landed on the cold ground. All around me, bodies lay awkwardly across the field. Most had their throats ripped out, while others had a giant hole where their heart should be.

What the fuck happened here? What's happening to me?

The crisp air stilled. My eyes locked on Rabon, and my body tensed in recognition. His mouth was traced in blood, his hands coated twice over. He stood at the edge of the field with a familiar smirk.

"You'll not escape me next time, brother," said Rabon.

A knock sounded behind me, washing the vision away, but the blood on my hands remained.

"Luke," Ember called from the other side of the door. "I know you're in there."

How could she know that? I'd come through the cafeteria door while she'd been on the first level.

"One second."

I rushed into the washroom and turned the sink knob to hot. With the blood scrubbed off, I looked at myself in the mirror. Blood-red irises stared back at me. I blinked several times, and they went back to their normal copper brown.

"Luke." Ember huffed, her voice muffled through the door.

I opened the door wide. "What is it?"

"We need to talk about earlier." She stepped into the

room and gestured toward my coffee table. "I'm pretty sure I got all of the broken glass, but you should be careful."

The steady rhythm of her heart accelerated.

"I acted rashly."

She wrapped her arms around herself, and her eyes bounced around the room, not wanting to connect with me. "Look, I'm sorry. I've had some time to think about that girl, and you were right. We couldn't have saved her."

I pulled her into my arms to calm her. "I shouldn't have taken her out like that. She wasn't attacking anyone."

Ember tilted her head back. "Maybe in the future, we can take a moment, just one, to assess if there's any way we can help these people?"

I nodded and released her. "I don't know a way to turn someone back from being a vampire, but it can't hurt to look into it."

She smiled, taking a step toward the door, and then scanned the room.

"What?"

"That book is gone. I can't find it," she sputtered. "I thought it would have some answers, but now it's gone."

I stepped closer to her, placing my hand on her shoulder. "Breathe."

She took in a big gulp of air and hiccuped.

"Where did you last see the book? And what does it look like?" I asked, taking my hand away.

She took another inhale before answering. "I brought

it back from Rabon's and sat it on one of the tables in the cafeteria. It's not there now, and Bob didn't know anything about it."

I nodded, backtracking to the corner of the room where I stacked my books and picked up the item she most wanted. She tried to take it from me, but I held it higher, just out of her grasp.

"Luke," she said, voice stern.

"It's a blank book." I lowered it, holding it closer to her.

"It's not blank," she said, grabbing the book from my hands. She flipped to a page. A blank page.

"See, blank," I said.

She shook her head, touching the page with the tip of her finger. Ink danced, swirling with magic as words appeared.

"Wow."

She bent her head to read the passage. "With the fall of Anu, our people will have peace before the cycle restarts." She paused briefly. "The tribes worry about Istros and his plans for revenge for his brother's death. I dare not tell a soul that he delivered the bloodline to me. And I promised my son that I would watch over his daughter."

I tensed at the name and pushed the book down to get Ember to look at me. *I should tell her what Rabon told me.*

"You see, it's not blank. I'm hopeful this will give me insights into my culture." She tilted her eyes back to the page. "If I can learn more about Rabon and Istros, I can figure out how to kill them." She smiled up at me.

My body tensed.

"What's wrong?" she asked.

"Nothing."

"Are you sure? You've been acting pretty weird."

"I'm fine," I said, and she smiled one last time before heading out.

I closed the door, flipped the switch, and sank onto my bed. I listened as Ember's feet padded down the hallway, up the stairs, and into the nurse's station above my room.

She'd been back a few months now since she first showed up out of the blue at one meeting and joined our dysfunctional monster-hunting group. She worked alongside Kaity and found those missing girls in days. Compared to the law enforcement and myself, she'd more than proven herself capable. She'd been a good asset to the team, even if she hardly used her abilities, but I understood that as well. Her father brainwashed her into believing that using her magic was the devil's work, and it still lingered with her. I'd never liked him, but I didn't hate him until the day he drove her away from me.

"She's not coming. She's already gone." Ellington shrugged, slipping Ember's pretty pink phone into his pocket. "She left this morning."

That couldn't be true. When she said yes to marrying me, I knew she meant it, but self-doubt crept in. I realized she had never messaged back this morning. I'd been too busy preparing for this moment.

Mr. Ellington stepped forward after the judge had left. "I'm sorry, son."

I knew he wasn't.

He removed her from my life mere moments before we were to start our lives together. I shrugged off the memory. I knew now that her father had talked her into leaving that day, and we had both moved on since. But being with her now gave me a serenity I didn't understand. I was grateful for our time apart—the time we needed to grow as individuals.

Thanks to my enhanced hearing, it was hard to ignore Ember's heavy footsteps pacing upstairs. After saving Hannah and almost dying, she'd come home to her heartless father. God, Ellington had been an asshole that day. She should have done more than torch that box. Ellington had shut his life off to his daughter. The look of hurt in Em's eyes tore at my dark heart, and the pleas in her voice almost made me wish I could teach that son of bitch a lesson.

I was still completely shocked I hadn't attacked Ellington as he walked out of the school, leaving Ember sobbing. But I was proud of her for finally standing up to him. It needed to happen if she was to ever have a life of her own. Em had changed so much. She now went by her given name, something she had told me in hushed tones under the high school bleachers like her father might somehow overhear her.

Since I had become a vampire, very little gave me the kind of peace she brought to the group.

Was I a real vampire? Or was I something darker?

Something wicked. It was always on the tip of my tongue to tell the rest of the gang about what happened on the balcony that night. Rabon believes I am a Chaos Brother—someone who had reigned with terror for centuries over supernaturals, slaughtered Ember's people, and destroyed so many others.

The images of the nightmare came floating back to the surface, and I pinched the bridge of my nose. *How could it have been real?* Yet the blood on my skin had washed down the drain.

The day Rabon had held Ember in his arms, my instinct kicked in. Before I knew what I was doing, I had jumped off the balcony after her. I hadn't made a conscious decision to do it. My body had acted on reflex.

She had saved both of us from plummeting into the ocean. I touched my arm where the lightning had burned into my skin. It was lighter than the rest but had healed. No matter what, I could not be a Chaos Brother because I could never leave her. It was like our connection was eternal—like I needed to protect her.

But she didn't need my protection. She'd found someone else for that. And if their scents were to be believed, then Christo could have the job. *Why am I still so connected to her?*

"Ah." I rolled over, pulling a pillow over my head to block out the thin line of light coming under the door, and drifted off to sleep.

Eight

EMBER

I sat down on the futon and opened the book to the first page. Like the others, it appeared to be blank, but touching it didn't make words appear.

"Hmm."

I flipped the page and touched that one. Words slid onto the faded cream parchment, creating lists of names. I skimmed them, but only a few stuck out. *Serafina. Is that my gran? Was this a family tree of my ancestors?*

I turned the page, and it continued for several more. Halfway down the fourth, the last name was written. Makani. I ran my thumb across her name. *My fucking history.* I followed my mother's line back. It sprouted from Serafina and shot down to my aunt, Lyanni. There were also blank spaces under my mother and Lyanni.

I devoured every name from all the pages. Turning, reading, flipping back and rereading the information. The section after was a collection of events, and it was from there that I had read the passage to Luke. I backed up a few pages and read aloud.

"A day of celebration, the soothsayer's words brought grim tidings. Her warning echoed through the packed halls of Anu that day. '*A Zodian born of this bloodline will end the Chaos.*' By nightfall, the whispers had spread. The prophecy had reached the brothers. Queen Dali summoned the tribes, ordering their strongest knights to secure their bloodline."

I leafed to the middle of the book. The entry before the last one described the night the Anu fell. Tear-streaked stains splotched the page as if the author had cried uncontrollably while writing. But the information confirmed what Sofia and Jasmine had told me weeks ago.

The following page actually seemed to be blank. The title on the opposite page was curious. *Truth Circle.* The circle that emerged onto the page was intricate in design. Pieces of it reminded me of the birthmarks on Sofia and Jasmine.

I put the book down, flattening the pages back so I could get a look at the circle. It was the birthmarks intertwined together. Sofia's was at the top, with Jasmine's on the west side. That had to mean the other symbols depicted were the other elements. Water, Fire, Earth, and Air. The center symbol was comparable to the one on my skin but lacked some of the lines. *Could this be aether?*

I read farther. The author described how to wield the elements to make an imprint of the circle on the ground.

It said that this spell was created by a tribe member of the thirteenth and was used by the queen to instill justice among its people. The key to making it work was the power in the imprint. I read and reread the passages. This circle would make the accused tell the truth or cause them pain.

In theory, if someone could withstand the pain, then they could lie, but the way the passage was worded made it sound impossible for the accused to be released without stating the truth. It seemed brutal. The only other way to release the spell was to kill the caster.

The page after had a title I'd remembered from Sofia and Jasmine's story: A Great Circle. It determined the leadership of Zodians. The book described it just the way they had. It also went into detail about the two that had been witnessed in Zodian history. The circle could only be made with all five elements present. And while a truth circle had to be made under the accused, only a willing Zodian could walk into the great circle. It couldn't be broken until only one was left. The rest either forfeited or died.

I flipped through a few more pages, and a list appeared, spanning the rest of the book. Each entry had a Roman numeral followed by random numbers. *Coordinates?* I grabbed my phone and typed the numbers into the map app. A location in London pinged. *Yes!*

I skipped to the last page and typed the last one in the list into the app. A place outside of Berkeley came up.

"Are these places that Zodians would meet?"

But when did they meet? Or had they already? I tried

rearranging the rest of the numbers in the sequence, but nothing made sense. I didn't see a date or a time. *How do I figure this out?*

I swiped away the app, and the home screen appeared on my phone. A photo of me and Dad from when I'd graduated appeared, and my heart ached. Pushing the contacts icon, I hit Dad's and waited. It rang and rang. Finally it rolled to voicemail like the last seventeen times.

"Dad, this is Em again. We need to talk. Call me back." I hung up.

The aether swirled with the scent of Jimmy Choo cologne, making me smile.

"Hey," I said without looking at Christo.

He sat down behind me, rubbing soothing circles into my back. He propped his head on my shoulder. *What's in the book?* he asked through our link.

A history of Zodians, I answered, leaning back into his body.

His fingers slid underneath the hem of my shirt, and heat pulsed through me. The mere rasp of his fingers sent my entire body aflame.

It's late, I said.

He kissed the side of my neck. *I guess it's a good thing you're still awake.*

Before I knew it, we were no longer at the school.

⊱──────⊰

I sighed and closed my eyes. I should have gone to bed when Christo brought me back, but instead, I'd read the history of my people again. It was the closest I'd come so far to learning about who I was. There were other elemental spells aside from the circle, and I devoured all of it. But now, unsheathing Warrior and trying to balance with it for the last hour, I'd wished I'd slept longer. I took a long, deep breath.

Practice holding the sword. You may not think it's heavy now, but in a long battle, it will be. Christo's voice penetrated the silence in my head.

I exhaled, closing my eyes to relax, but the darkness brought back the dead eyes of the scared teenage girl. She'd been a vampire. That had been clear when her head had landed in front of me and turned to dust, but it had hurt that Luke didn't wait until we could research some way to possibly save her. I'd promised to help, but I never even had a chance to try.

Gasping, I dropped my stance and sank to my knees on the practice mat. I released the sword, bringing my hands to my chest. My heart pounded against my palm. Guilt settled in my stomach once again. I closed my eyes and tried to clear her wide eyes from my thoughts.

"You need more practice," Christo said.

Low in my core, something fluttered at the sound of his voice. My thoughts were replaced with images that made my face flame. I kept my eyes closed, tracking Christo's movements.

He circled around me, but I could sense the smile on

his lips. We had spent several hours enjoying each other the night before.

"I know," I said.

He stopped on my left, squatting down to my level, and waited for me to open my eyes before talking. "Remember, your sword is an extension of yourself."

I groaned, having heard that same phrase from Luke and Lyra.

Luke had grown up interested in weapons, taking classes and finally deciding he enjoyed boxing. His state champion trophy had sat proudly in his room, the youngest person in his division to win that title. Now it collected dust in a house he no longer visited but couldn't bring himself to sell.

"Your thoughts mingle with his name on them."

I raised my head at Chris's words. *His name is Luke. I can't help that we live together.*

"We could live together," Christo said.

I shook my head. *Stop snooping in my thoughts! You promised.*

"I know, and I'll try, but we need to spend more time together." He pressed closer. "Wouldn't you like that?" he asked, voice breathless.

"I—" My body relaxed as I stared into his blue eyes.

I went in for a kiss, but Christo stood and backed away from me, breaking our connection.

Luke came through the door a second later.

I was grateful that Chris respected my wishes, even though he complained every time we were together and continuously prompted me to tell my friends the truth.

I climbed to my feet, picking up the sword and sheathing it.

Luke came to stand by me.

"Hey," I said.

"Hey," Luke said, glancing at Chris. "What are you doing here?"

Chris cocked his head.

Through our bond, I caught vague snippets of attitude, and *I could take you to school* . . . before Chris blocked me out.

Chris raised his eyebrow at me before turning back to Luke. "I have the maps of the nests you asked about."

Luke grabbed the roll of paper from Chris's outstretched hand. He headed to the side of the room where a fold-out table was set up and rolled out the map of Happy Valley. Using discarded weights and my sword, he flattened the corners.

"This is pretty detailed."

Chris shrugged. "It's all I could do on short notice, but some of them aren't active."

Luke nodded and continued to stare at the map.

Chris turned to me, nodded, and then disappeared.

"What is that?" I asked, stepping up to the table.

Luke scanned the gym and then turned his attention back to me. "I asked Christo to look for vampire nests in Happy Valley. The church had to have been one. There were blankets lying about and wood stacked in piles around the altar. I wondered how many more there could be in town."

"Oh," I said, looking down at all the circles. "There's

a lot." Most of them were in older parts of town where few people lived.

"Yep." Luke rolled the paper up. "I'll have to determine which ones are still active and then plan an attack to annihilate them." He started for the gym's exit, deep in thought.

"Bye," I said, but he was already gone.

Eyeing the sword on the edge of the table, I unsheathed it once more and started on a set of workouts Luke had shown me several days ago. While I would have rather been taking a nap, I knew this was important. I needed to improve enough to save a girl—or anyone—before there was any more suffering.

Nine

EMBER

Nothing in the last month had made much sense. It all started when Chris handed over those bloody maps to Luke. Since then he's hung out with the demons playing poker almost every night. Chris would come in laughing with Ted and Kaity after patrolling. The one good outcome of it all was that Luke came out of his room to oversee the game from a stool at the bar. If I had been new, it would look like they were old friends.

I should've be happy my secret boyfriend was in fact getting along with my friends. I mean, that was what he wanted. Christo wanted me to be open about us, and if my friends seemed to like him, then all the better. I *could* be honest and tell them the truth, but there was a small amount of resentment left about the way he bonded with me. That's what held me back from telling my friends. What if they abandoned me like Dad?

I still didn't understand why Dad changed the locks and packed up all my stuff. *But I was all I had.* I needed to be strong in the field and able to do my job at the bank —it was my only source of income, and I needed it now more than ever.

Trying to keep up with patrols, taking shifts at the bank to keep my day job, using every spare moment to practice, and not getting enough sleep wasn't working for me. So today, I called in sick for the afternoon to take a nap. And almost like magic, I got the night off from patrol. I was determined to get some rest.

Instead of napping, I sat on the futon cross-legged, eyeing the box Dad had kept hidden for the past sixteen years. I stared at the box before me, wishing it would open, but nothing happened. There were no seams. There were no screws or nails or clamps around the edges.

No lock or hinges. The entire thing was wood.

And that therein was the problem.

The symbol matching my birthmark was inlaid into the top of the box.

Dad had flipped out several months ago. My left hand reached involuntarily toward my right wrist, where my bracelet lay. I had worn it every day except *that day*. I hesitated, my fingers brushing across the clasp. Instead, I massaged the leather and took a deep breath. *Did this box hold anything special?* Maybe it was just a pretty box with nothing inside. My head fell forward, and I took two deep breaths. I couldn't squash the feeling that it held something dear to me. That it was mine and I needed to open it. But how?

I rolled out of bed and walked toward the blackout

window, wishing I could see the sunlight outside. This should be easy. But now that Dad had stopped talking to me, there was no other way to get answers about my mother's past. I had already read that entire book I stole from Rabon's, but there wasn't anything personal about my family. This box could hold my mother's secrets. *Or it was empty.* I didn't know and would not know until I actually got it open.

I flicked my wrist, sending air toward the box, smirking as it rolled across the futon. Symbols on the box glowed bright. I rushed to catch it before it fell to the floor. My mouth hung open, but as I sat back on the bed, the glow faded. *Did it react to my powers?*

"Fucking genius," I whispered, sitting beside the box again.

I took a deep breath, sending a small wave of air toward the box, not enough to move it but the right amount for the light show.

A few more times yielded the same results.

Standing up once more, I paced around the room. What else could make it open? Air had been my mother's strongest element. Earth could be the key, but there was no dirt here to use, and I had yet to really test those abilities. I didn't want to accidentally collapse the building.

Stopping in the middle of the room, I closed my eyes and focused. There was something I wasn't getting. The symbol carved into the box was the same symbol marking my wrist.

With my eyes still closed, I unclasped the leather

bracelet, letting it fall to the floor. I hadn't really inspected the birthmark closely in so long. In high school, I had taken the bracelet off on occasion to view it and to feel closer to my mother. That had stopped when my father caught me one afternoon looking at it. *"Emma, what are you doing? Cover that up at once!" He had shouted, rushing into my room.*

I looked down at the symbol.

What does this all mean?

I sat back down on the futon, making the metal scrap against the floor from my weight. Leaning back, I saw a flash of light flicker.

The box was glowing, but so was my mark.

Were they connected?

I moved my hand closer to the box, but there was no glow. I flipped my wrist.

"Just work, please," I uttered.

Using the aether, I wrapped it around the box, searching for its own thread. The glow was faint, but the closer I moved my wrist to the box, the brighter it got. A click sounded, and the box sprang open. The light faded from the room.

The box lay open in front of me. *I did it. I figured it out.* Even if it happened by accident. It's a win for sure.

I reached into the box, greedy to finally connect with something of my mother's. But my effort was met with a cut. I examined the slice. Tiny drops of blood smeared over my fingers. I peered inside, identifying what had slashed me. I pulled out a knife. The blade was similar to my mother's sword. *A companion.* I laid it aside and pulled the next items out. One receipt and a picture.

Setting the receipt to the side, I perused the picture. Two young girls squinted up at me. Smiling, dressed in Sunday best. The same mark was visible on both their wrists. This had to be my mother and her sister, but which one was which? I had never actually seen the full profile of my mother before since the photo hanging in the hallway was taken from the back. Dad had been too grieved to have them floating around the house.

I stared at the picture for what seemed like hours. A knock sounded at my door. I scooped up all the contents I had taken out and put them back into the box. Closing the lid, a snap echoed in the room.

Sprinting to the door, I raised my right hand to pull the handle, noticing my bare wrist.

"One second," I yelled, backtracking to the center of the room. I pulled the bracelet over my wrist and secured it. "Come in."

Grace barged into the room, trapping me in a hug. "I missed you. Luke said you didn't go to work. Are you feeling okay?"

"For the most part. I've been really tired lately and thought a nap would be better than going to work."

Grace's smile grew. "That's for sure. I call out all the time."

I shook my head. She was one of four legal assistants at her father's firm, which made her super bored at work with nothing to do.

"What are you doing here?"

"I was going to head to Portland and do some shopping."

I glanced at the box. *I'm so close.* "That sounds fun. I hope you have a good time."

She humphed. "Damn, I was hoping you wanted to go with me."

I shook my head. "Not today."

"Poo, what about Friday night? My parents are going on another trip." Grace rolled her eyes.

"It's cute that they're still madly in love with each other," I said, leaning against the white-washed wall.

Grace shook her head. "They're always TMI and think I don't see it. It's really gross."

I laughed. "I can come over. What time?"

"I'm going to the Collective after work at five, so maybe seven. Can you bring pizza, or do you want to grab tacos?" She asked, starting toward the door.

"Pizza. I'm sure I can get Bob to make us some drinks, too."

"Yay! It's a date." She disappeared in a ball of her light.

Alone in my room again, I sat down on the futon. After removing my bracelet once more, I opened the box within seconds.

I carefully pulled out the knife this time and laid it on the bedside table. The picture came next, but I took a good look at the receipt.

Anita's Curiosities. It listed the phone number, date of purchase, and address and was stamped "paid." But the receipt wasn't for the knife, it was for a gown worth

$1200.00. *Wow, that's one expensive gown. Had it been my mother's?*

Setting that aside, I grabbed my phone and turned on the flashlight. Pointing it into the box, I saw one last item. A book wedged into the compartment. I pulled it out. It was similar to the one that sat on my table. I opened the pages, but they were not blank. Words filled the book cover to cover, even in the margins, written sideways at the top. *A journal?*

After reading the first couple of pages, I would have bet my life it belonged to my mother. It had sections devoted to her thoughts on my father.

There's a look in his eyes that tells me he's not being honest with me about something, but I don't know what. I wish my mother hadn't gone radio silent on me. I could ask her to brew me a truth spell. I'm not sure if she would like him or not. He's sweet, charming, and beautiful.

It was this entry at the beginning that confirmed that this book belonged to Mom.

He almost walked right past me today, except the sun came out of the clouds, gleaming across the land, and my breath held. I gazed upon a sword I had never actually seen but heard about in stories. He neared me, carrying the sword across his back, and my heart beat rapidly. The sun caught on the poorly wrapped blade. My soul had called out to it, and it had called to me. I stopped the man wielding the sword and accused him of stealing it from my family. The look on his face, priceless, but he challenged me all the same. I laughed and told him I could split the sword into two. He laughed at me, a hearty, warm sound that made me blush under the hot summer sun, but he played along. I took the sword from his grasp, my heart beating faster at the touch of our fingers. Clasping the hilt of the sword, I breathed in and out for a few seconds before summoning the blade to do my bidding. His eyes wide, he gazed upon not one but two swords in my hands.

My mother wrote this in her own hand. The same story my father had once told me about their first meeting. I ran my fingers over the passage before glancing at the sword that drew them together.

"Ember," a voice called from outside my door.

I jerked up, noticing that the shutters on the window were gone. It was dark outside. The game with the demons. I had gotten lost in my mother's words, thumbed halfway through the journal, and learned so much. So much that my father had refused to tell me.

"Ember," Luke said with more persistence.

"Yeah?" I asked.

"Are you coming down to the game?"

I eyed the journal. I didn't have to patrol tonight, and the excitement of reading my mother's personal thoughts wouldn't go away. "No, I'll catch the next one," I yelled back.

I sat waiting for a reply, and when none came, I connected with the aether. From under the door, I could sense that Luke was walking away.

I laid the book on the table and returned the rest of the items to the box. I rushed through my nighttime routine so I could climb into bed and read late into the night. Mom's adventures came first.

Ten

EMBER

Training with Lyra over the phone was not the easiest. I huffed, closing my eyes, trying to concentrate on my breathing.

"This takes a lot of energy. If you feel exhausted, don't attempt to do this. You could pull yourself close to death."

Duly noted. I had collapsed and slept for hours after my last attempts.

"Keep breathing in sync and clear your mind. Think only of your destination."

I counted slowly, inhaling and exhaling, clearing my mother's latest journal entries from my mind. She'd been uncertain if moving in with my father would be the right decision and had debated it for six months.

Breathe in, breathe out—clear everything from my mind.

I envisioned myself standing on the opposite side of the range, down by the lights that weren't working. Lyra's voice sounded far away. I only had my destination in mind.

"When you can clearly see where you want to go, draw forth the energy into yourself and release the energy back into the universe but with yourself."

She makes it sound so easy.

I released one final breath before inhaling the electricity that surrounded me. No one ever noticed it floating around in the aether. Taking it all in, I held it, feeling the strength, and then released it. My stomach dropped quickly, and my muscles spasmed. Opening my eyes, I stood forty feet away from where I started.

Jumping, I yelled, "I did it."

Crap. Lyra couldn't hear me from here. I started across the range.

Wait, I could use Agni again, clear my mind. I stood, letting go of my accomplishment, and inhaled the energy. Except, when I released it, I remained in the same spot. *That didn't work.*

Again I clenched my fist, freeing my mind from all thoughts, but nothing happened. I trudged back to the awning, and on my approach, I could hear Lyra shouting.

"Are you okay? What happened? Are you there? Where did you go?"

"I'm here, sorry," I said, picking up the phone and sitting on one of the stone benches. "It worked, but I couldn't come back."

"The fact that you got it to work is amazing. You're the only one who can do this."

"Are you sure?"

"It's a lost art form. The last person I knew who could do it was my mother."

"*Your* mother?" I asked.

Lyra hardly talked about her past. She kept herself closed off from the world.

"Yes, she was extremely powerful. Remember that your powers are affected by your moods and energy. Are you running?" She asked, and I told her I tried to get it in every week, but I had a lot going on and I highly doubted she would count the number of times I had to run after vampires. "Running will help with endurance and keeping your strength up."

"Thanks, Lyra."

"No problem, kiddo. I'll call back in a few weeks to check in on your progress. Maybe then you can travel here to see me."

"That would be nice." I told her bye and pocketed my phone.

If Agni became easy, like creating a fireball, then I would be able to visit anyone. I missed my friend's comedic outlook of the world.

I got up and stretched, checking the time, when a bright light flashed in front of me.

"Hey, Kaity," I said when she came into focus. "Perfect timing. I finished training with Lyra for today."

She fluffed out her clothes. "How is it going? Any better?"

I had mentioned my struggles to master this technique to her. "I actually was able to do it today. I traveled over to the targets." I pointed, and she turned to look in that direction. "But I was only able to do it once."

"That's progress. I've searched my family spell book, and there isn't a spell that will let you travel through lightning. It must be specific to Zodians."

"Possibly. Are you ready?"

She nodded and stepped farther into the grass. I followed, making sure I was equal distance from her and the pavilion. Once in place, she manifested a fireball and threw it my way.

Dodging, I summoned my fire into a small ball, throwing it at Kaity. It missed her, and we continued to fire at each other, but there was no clear victor. The sun beat down upon us, and sweat soaked my shirt. Kaity never quit a practice session until one of us went down. My sore knees and throbbing feet told me we'd been doing this for a while.

Christo's voice filtered through my head. *Why are you dodging her fireballs?*

Cringing, I ducked. *Get out of my head.*

Answer me.

What do you want me to do?

I sidestepped one of Kaity's attempts. The sandy terrain made my foot slide, and I sank down to my knee, rolling out of the way of another.

Get out of my head so I can focus.

Why dodge when you could catch?

I stopped dead. It must have shocked Kaity because she stopped too before deciding to throw three fireballs at once.

I could catch them. Fire doesn't hurt me. It was my weapon of choice.

I took a breath, releasing the aether to help me determine the exact moment I should catch them.

Bringing my hands forward, I caught the first one. Shock rippled across Kaity's face before I flung it back at her. Catching the last two, I did the same. Kaity stood stunned. The first one hit her in the stomach, knocking her down. The second and third flew past on each side of her head.

"Wow," she yelled. "It never occurred to me to do that. Makes sense."

I crossed over to her, reaching my hand out to help her stand. "Me either. I guess I could have saved us training time if I had figured it out sooner."

"Nah," she sputtered, running her hands through her hair. "My ends are burned." Her eyes widened, light surrounded her, and a moment later, she was gone.

"Sorry," I said into the air.

Christo materialized beside me. "You're improving."

I nodded, going over to the stone table where my towel and water were.

"You need to use your powers more when you fight," Christo said.

I took a drink of water before answering. "I'm learning."

I used the aether all the time. Mostly without actively thinking about it. It was a constant tickle providing me information on my surroundings. But fire was on another level. I grew up thinking it was bad. My dad squashed that side of me. Lyra had helped at the beginning, teaching me how to control my emotions to keep the fire from hurting anyone. Now Kaity was helping me learn how to fight with it. I'd slowly started to incorporate it in my hand-to-hand combat during patrols and practices with Luke. Especially since his eyes had changed.

I picked up my gear and placed it back into my bag. He grabbed my jacket and handed it to me.

I gave him a sideways glance. "Why did you stop by?"

I was concerned. How are you feeling today? You've been exhausted over the last few weeks.

I listened to his voice, that calming influence in the back of my head, and nodded in his direction. The bond connected him with my emotional state. I opened my car door and chucked the bag inside.

He leaned against the metal, a frown on his face. "I lost the game last night."

I laughed. "Sorry, it's just that I kept hearing your thoughts when you were playing with them a few days ago. Your thought kept repeating." Chuckling again, I covered my mouth, hoping to dim down my jolly. Smiling, I managed to deepen my voice. "I will not lose to these underlings." And then I burst into a full belly laugh.

"Yeah, well, I'm not certain they didn't cheat."

"Nah, they wouldn't do that." I stepped between his legs. "Bob, Chase, and Scout would never cheat."

My smile widened. Our bodies molded together.

He raked his eyes over my body, telling me exactly what he wanted was exactly what I craved.

Eleven

EMBER

I sat cross-legged on the floor of Grace's room. There was barely enough space to walk, much less for a sleepover. We'd been doing them since Dad allowed me to stay the night. The first time had been back in middle school. I always chose to come over to Grace's home instead of staying at mine. The fact that my room had been bigger didn't dampen the experiences we had in her room, especially since Dad wasn't present.

Grace had all four walls decorated with furniture that butted against each other—vanity, bed, bookshelf, standing jewelry case, and a closet overfilled with clothes that spilled into the small space. In the middle of her room, we had laid down some old quilts. I honestly didn't think I'd ever seen her room clean.

I chewed on the strawberry candy rope I'd snatched from the kitchen on my way up. Grace pulled clothes after clothes out of her closet, holding them to her body before shaking her head and flinging them onto an ever-growing pile. She had another date with the cute redhead from Eats! this weekend and couldn't decide what to wear.

She plopped down on the makeshift blanket and flung the mini skirt back onto the closet floor.

"You know whatever you wear will look good, but lighter colors always look better on you." I said, twirling the candy rope, "Something about your fair hair."

"I know you're right, and I want to wear something pink, but I can't decide which one," Grace said.

"You have the entire day tomorrow to figure this out, correct?"

She nodded because she had taken the day off to get ready. I shook my head, going back to devouring the candy. My father didn't see any benefit of housing candy when I was growing up and probably still didn't. I would only get special treats like this when I came over to Grace's, which made spending time with my best friend extra special.

We scarfed down the pizzas I picked up from town. We'd spent the last few hours going through options for Grace's date, taking sips out of the jug Bob had made for us. It tasted like blueberries and lemons.

"All right, what do you want to watch?" Grace asked.

It was a requirement for our sleepover tradition that watching a movie kept us up past midnight. Not that being up late wasn't a daily occurrence now, but back in junior high, even high school, it seemed totally cool.

"Let's watch a classic." I leaned back against the bed frame.

She leaned over to her bookshelf, which was in reach, and pulled a disk off. I didn't catch the title before she placed it into the player.

"Guess the title?" She smiled.

It was a game we used to play to see if we could guess the movie before it appeared on the screen. The movie started to play, zooming in on the setting, but I already knew what it was from the intro credits.

"*Pirates*," I giggled, one of our favorites.

She settled against her bed with me.

The movie continued, but my mind wandered back to the book I'd nabbed from Rabon's house. I was convinced that some of the blank pages would reveal words if I could figure out the magic to use.

"What's up? Your face is scrunched up," Grace asked, plucking one of the ropes out of my hand.

I eyed her, chewing. "Well, that was mine. And if you must know. I would really like to talk to Sofia and Jasmine but didn't get their numbers when they were here. I thought Kaity had since they stayed with her, but she didn't either."

"What do you want to ask them?"

I shrugged. "I just have some cultural questions about my people I was hoping they could answer. They gave me a rundown of some important events that happened, but I'm sure there's so much more I could learn from them."

Grace took a Post-it note off her haphazard bookshelf and a pen lying on the floor beside her. She then scrolled through her phone before writing a number down on the piece of paper.

"Here," she said, handing it to me.

"What is it?" I read the scrawl but didn't recognize the numbers.

"You wanted their numbers. This is Sofia's number."

My eyes snapped open, and I pulled Grace into a hug. "Thank you." I released her.

Now I can get somewhere with the book. And she would have much more information than just that. I stuffed the pink paper into the pocket of my jeans.

We watched most of the movie, the night drifting into the early morning, before speaking again. My eyes flicked over to Grace to check if she was still awake. Catching my eyes, she turned toward me.

"Do you know much about those demons?" Grace asked.

Not sure what she meant, I asked, "What demons?"

The screen was showing the end of the movie and would be over in a matter of minutes.

"The ones that hang out at the bar."

I rubbed my shoulder. "Not really, I guess. I've had dinner with them a few times, but they don't share much about their history."

"Luke should ask them to leave."

What? Alert, I stared at her. A look creased her face that didn't favor her appearance.

"What do you mean?"

"They are demons," she said slowly, like that explained everything.

"So," I prompted, "what does that matter?"

"Demons are evil." She pulled her arms around herself. "They aren't trustworthy."

"I'm not sure where you heard that, but it's not true. I mean, some demons are evil and can't be trusted, but it's not like they're all evil. Bob hasn't hurt anyone, and Luke said the other day he's been in Happy Valley a long time."

"Do you think he would tell us the truth if he *did* harm someone?"

"I—"

She cut me off before I could continue. "Right, they're evil and should be dealt with. Luke shouldn't allow them near him when he's sleeping. What if they tried to kill him during the day? He would have nowhere to run."

"If they wanted to kill him, they've had many opportunities to do so already."

I didn't understand where this fear of demons was coming from. Yes, we went out every night to keep the town safe, but we didn't harm any demons who kept their noses clean. Mostly we destroyed vampires who drained their victims. Vampires needed fresh blood to replenish their own rotting blood—without it, they would turn to ash.

She glanced at the screen, and my eyes followed. The movie had come to a close. She turned the TV off and lay down on the makeshift pallet we'd made earlier.

I lay down beside her, listening to her shallow breaths

as she drifted off to sleep, but I couldn't. I rolled over, poking her in the side.

When she was awake enough, I asked, "Why are you afraid of the demons at the bar?"

Her body shrugged, too deeply rooted in sleep to answer.

Could someone at her nighttime job have said something? I honestly didn't know much about the operation she worked for. *The Collective.* It sounded ominous but was supposed to be made up of other half angels like Grace.

Hopefully, in time, she would understand that not all supernaturals were evil. There was no black and white. What made a demon evil was their personality and the environment they surrounded themselves in. The old nature-versus-nurture debate.

Twelve

I was laid bare, naked in a field of the farm I would never again tend. My body burned, the blood sizzling before the skin healed over. The stars shone above me. My life was no longer my own.

"It's done," a voice said.

I turned, but nothing was there. I climbed to my feet, brushing the dirt from my arms. My brother lay unscathed like me, naked to the sky. His eyes blinked open.

"How are we alive?" I uttered.

Rabon stood. "I made a pact with the God of Darkness."

"Those men." I swiped my hair away from my eyes.

"They are the ones who killed us and your beloved."

"But why?" I asked.

Rabon put a hand on my shoulder. "You had no status. You sullied their sister."

A breeze filtered through the valley, and I searched

through the charred debris of the house for anything that survived. All was lost.

The shirts on a clothesline whipped in the night's wind. I walked over and grabbed some clothes. I picked up my trusted scythe and began my hunt. *They will pay.*

I caught up with them, surrounding a small campfire on a sandy beach under the bright full moon. They passed a flaggen around in silence as I approached from the west. The blade of my scythe gleamed under the moonlight. I weighed the weapon, swinging, and it breathed a whisper of death.

The flaggen and the arm holding it dropped onto the now crimson-covered sand.

They turned as one. The next cut went through the neck, his eyes wide as the head toppled to the beach.

"We killed you."

I spun around, twirling the scythe over my head and hooking the next murderer in the gut. I lifted him and tossed him into the flames.

"A ghost."

A sword was finally drawn against me, but I was stronger. My years of field labor proved a far greater advantage than their aristocratic lives.

Following the blade's momentum, I ran it into the next man, slicing through his chest and cutting downward, spilling his entrails to the ground.

I pulled back, the moon reflecting off my crimson blade.

The last murderer tried to flee the camp. I sliced through his groin, knocking him to his knees. I stepped forward and brought my blade around to his front, lifting his head to see the look of terror carved on his face.

"I am chaos," I whispered.

I brought the weapon toward me, slicing through his neck, releasing the head from its body.

Four brothers lay motionless on the beach, the fire dying out.

A voice filtered through the wind as the waves crashed upon the shore. *Good work.* The first words darkness spoke to me. Adrenaline coursed through my veins, energizing me to my soul.

I dropped my weapon to the beach. A sparkle in the darkness caught my attention. I bent down and retrieved the pendant attached to one headless body. I wiped the blood off the gift I had made her. *Tesia*

I raced along the shore back toward the village. As the buildings came into view, I slowed. *She is not gone.* I stood outside the house. The entryway was open with candles burning into the night. I took quick steps across the stone floor to the courtyard at the center of the home.

A sheer cloth lay upon the body. *No, God. Please no. Not Tesia.* I stepped up to the dais and ripped the sheet off. She lay immobile. Her eyes were covered with coins for her safe passage through the underworld. Her skin, a pale gray.

"Tesia," I whispered.

She'd been my heart.

⊱————⊰

I sat up in bed, sweating as the dream vanished. A movement caught my attention. I grabbed the assailant and pulled her to me. Her body was warm. She was alive. *My Tesia's alive.*

"Luke," Kaity yelped.

I nuzzled against her neck, breathing in her familiar scent as the words slipped through my mind. *Kaity.* I loosened my hands.

Kaity leaned back.

All I saw was Tesia's eyes.

"Luke," she whispered, and then gently kissed my lips.

I snaked my hands through her hair, pulling her closer, crushing her lips against mine. It was nice to have a warm body against me. Someone who loved me. Someone to block out all the blood. All the chaos. I pulled her body over mine, bucking into her as she groaned. She reached to pull off her top, and I released her hair as she flung her shirt to the floor. I grabbed the straps of her bra and ripped, pulling her to me again and scraping my teeth along her lower lip. She whimpered against me, grinding her hips against my erection.

"Luke," Kaity moaned into my mouth.

She climbed out of the bed, breaking the connection, and slid her pants off.

I swiveled, lowering my feet to the ground as Kaity climbed into my lap. Her folds were soaked as she rubbed against me. She positioned herself, but I grabbed a handful of hair, bringing her to a stop. I pulled her head back, exposing her breast to my mouth, and sucked on the pert nipple. She whimpered, and I slipped two fingers into her pussy, stroking and petting her as I devoured her breast.

"Please," she begged.

I brought her lips to mine as I thrust into her. We groaned together as she started to ride me, digging her nails into my skin as she bucked. I twisted my hand in her hair, making her go faster. Kaity cried out as a flood of her juices ran down my leg and her body spasmed around my cock. I grunted, thrusting hard one last time before I came.

I slipped my fingers from her hair, falling back against the bed. The door creaked open. Ember's wide eyes found mine.

"Oh my gosh, I'm so sorry," she cried out, slapping her hand over her eyes. "I'll just leave."

She backed out of the room as Kaity scrambled off me, pulling a sheet around herself.

After the door shut, Kaity hugged the cover tighter. She stood in the shadows of the room.

"Kaity," I said, standing and reaching for a pair of pants. *Shit, what have I done?*

"This is so embarrassing," Kaity whispered, coming out of the corner. She picked up her clothes from the floor. "How am I going to face her now?"

At her cheerful tone, I risked a look at her face. *This was a mistake.* I should have pushed her away when she kissed me. But . . . I rubbed the sleep from my eyes. I'd been caught up in the dream. *Tesia. Who was she?*

Kaity had pulled most of her clothes on when she

sank down on the bed. Leaning in, she tried to kiss my cheek, but I pulled away.

"What's wrong?" she asked.

I closed my eyes, wanting to delay this conversation, but it couldn't wait.

"This was a mistake," I said, cringing on the words. *That is not what I should have said.*

"A mistake?" she whispered, leaning away from me.

"I didn't mean it like that."

She stood up, marching across the room to pull on her sandals. "Then how did you mean it, Luke?" Her voice hardened from the hurt.

That isn't what I wanted. I wanted her to be happy. Because there was no future for us. I was a vampire or something much worse. There was no way we could be together. She would want children. *Heck, how could I be a parent when I can't even go outside in the sunlight?*

We'd met before I turned, but we'd always had trust issues. Kaity had lied about being a witch. And her mother had always warned her not to tell anyone. I could always tell she was holding back from me. Over our two year relationship, it was just one of the reasons we broke up so many times.

I guess I always knew we weren't perfect for each other in those early years. But she had been there for me after Ember left, even though she was just a rebound at the time, I thought.

"I shouldn't have kissed you back," I said at last.

Her hands were clenched in front of her, wringing her fingers together as she looked at me. "But we're so good together. And I love you. You did kiss me back. It means something." Her voice rose with each word.

She was on the verge of tears now.

I stood up to console her, but she moved back against the door.

"No, Luke," she whispered. "You do love me."

"I do love you, Kaity, but I'm different now, and that's why we can't be together."

She wailed, "You can't mean that. It's not true. We can work through this."

I clenched my hands together. "Kaity, I'm sorry this was a big misunderstanding."

"You're sorry," she repeated. "I can't believe you would fuck me only to tell me you no longer love me. You're full of shit, Luke." She half turned, tears in her eyes. "So. There's no reason to try?"

I shook my head. "No, you could find someone so much better than me."

"You, Luke Bowen, are an ass." She flung the words at me and rushed out of the room.

The door bounced off the concrete wall.

I stood frozen as I listened to her steps echo through the school until the front door opened and slammed shut. She was gone.

I am an ass. She didn't know the half of it.

I walked into the shower and turned on the hot water, washing away my sins. As if I could. Her face when she realized I hadn't died in the car accident that took my parents filled my mind. She was elated even though, at the time, we weren't dating. But I had agreed the day before the accident to give her a chance to explain herself.

She told me later that she had planned on telling me about her abilities, but with the wreck and then her mother's passing, months went by before we had a moment alone to talk about all the events that had happened.

It didn't matter now. But I knew back then that being a vampire would prevent us from having a future together. She had to realize that at some point. There were so many obstacles in our way. Including the chaos inside me.

Thirteen

LUKE

After changing into some workout clothes, I headed to find Ember. I took a moment outside my room to listen to the voices in the building. I could hear the demons talking shit to each other, but above me was a steady beat. I headed for the gym.

Stepping into my second home, I stood at the edge of the mat, watching Ember practice movements with her sword. The day I lost control seemed to give her a sense of confidence with her abilities, even if she didn't fully believe it yet. She'd excelled at incorporating her magic with sword fighting.

"Where's Kaity?" Ember asked, jerking me out of my thoughts.

"She's upset and went home," I said, walking to her. "Do you want to spar with me? Isn't that what you had planned with her?"

Ember nodded, and she took a deep breath before positioning herself.

I bent my knees and brought my fists up.

She frowned.

"What?"

"Aren't you going to grab a weapon?"

"Nah. And you should use your powers like you would with Kaity."

She nodded, sheathing her sword and setting it off to the side before walking back onto the mat. She brought her hands up, her fists glowing. The gym buzzed with energy, and the hair on my arms rose. I could feel the heat radiating off her, a stark contrast to the chaos coursing through my veins.

I clenched my fists, readying myself. Ember lunged forward with a burst of flames scorching the air around me. Dodging and weaving, I searched for an opening as heat licked at my skin.

My fists blurred as I unleashed a barrage of punches, each blow landing with a satisfying thud. Quick to retaliate, Ember conjured walls of flames, keeping me at bay. But I refused to be intimidated, pressing forward with unrelenting determination.

The heat was intense, and sweat began pouring down my brow as I battled against the elemental force before me. Ember danced away from my attacks, her movements fluid and graceful, like flames flickering in the wind. I channeled every ounce of strength and skill I possessed into my anger from earlier. *I will not be outmatched.*

Ember unleashed a torrent of fire, the flames burning my skin, threatening to consume me. But I did not give into the fear, pushing through the inferno with sheer force of will. With a final, bone-crushing punch, I sent all my strength into an undercut, willing Ember to give up. My fist met air, and I came crashing down to the ground. I gazed up to find Ember standing over me, her hand ablaze before my face. *I lost. Again.*

Fourteen

EMBER

I wiped the sweat from that workout off my face as I entered the adjoining bathroom of my room. The look on Luke's face after I beat him was priceless. Whatever his problems were, it would help if he would get his act together with Kaity. I'd seen the way he looked at her when he thought no one was paying attention.

If Dad would get his shit together, then everything would be just peachy.

"Jump, dance, let's make sweet love tonight."

Jolted by Grace's singing, I let out a breath when I noticed the noise was coming from my phone on the coffee table.

"Jump, dance, let's make sweet love tonight."

Grimacing at Grace's sleepover prank, I picked up my phone. "Childish, really childish," I muttered.

When I caught a glimpse of the caller ID, I almost dropped it back on the table.

Dad.

Dad's calling.

I didn't have long before the call went to voicemail. I tried to answer, missing the accept button the first and second time. *Deep breaths.*

"Hello," I said, placing it beside my ear, then pulling it away, watching sweat run down my arm. *Gross.* I laid the phone on the table, hitting the speaker button before trying again. "Hey, Dad, I'm so glad you called."

"Em, I've gotten your messages, and yes, we need to talk." His voice seemed distant.

"Yes, I want to tell you how sorry I am for the choices I've made over the last couple of years."

Cutting me off, he said, "Not now. Can we meet at the range tomorrow night? Shoot a few rounds like old times?"

"Of course. What time do you want to meet?" I asked, knowing it would be dark early tomorrow, and the range had yet to repair its broken lights that got shot out earlier in the year.

"The lights are up and running, and I have meetings until six. How about seven?"

"Oh, okay, I'll be there," I said, clenching my hand to my chest.

Happiness spread before I heard the click. Looking down at the phone, I saw that he ended the call. *Tomorrow.* We would be able to talk through this like adults.

Everything seemed to be coming up Ember. Lying

back in bed, I drifted off to sleep, knowing that our conversation tomorrow could solidify our relationship again. He had to forgive me so we could move on to look forward to the future as a family.

Fifteen

EMBER

"Jump, dance. Let's make sweet love tonight" sang in my ear as I rolled over, trying to turn the noise off. I'd forgotten to change the ringtone before falling asleep last night. Pushing the side button, silencing the noise, I tried to sleep a little longer.

There was no reason for me to get up early today. No work or patrol later tonight. The only item on my list today was to talk with Dad at the range. We were going to shoot a round of archery and have a serious conversation about me and my abilities.

Shit, we're going shooting.

I bolted up in bed. My bow had been destroyed. Lost in the cave. And the one Christo gifted me had been damaged the night Kit attacked me. I'd tried using it, but the arrows never shot straight. I didn't have one for tonight. There was no way I could find a custom-made replacement on such short notice. And I wouldn't be able to use my father's. *Double shit.*

Squeezing my eyes shut, I tried to think of a solution.

"Jump, dance. Let's make sweet love tonight."

My phone buzzed again. Lighting up the screen, I could see that I had several missed calls. Three from Ted in the last thirty minutes. *What could he possibly want at nine in the morning?*

"Hello," I said.

"Ember, have you seen Luke?"

"No," I said. "I'm not his keeper, you know."

"You both live in the same building and are mere hallways apart."

I rolled my eyes. "Still doesn't make me his keeper. He's probably still asleep," I said, trying to remember if he went out on patrol last night after our sparring match.

"He's not answering his phone. It's rolling straight to voicemail, which doesn't happen. With super hearing, he hates listening to a ringing phone."

"What do you want me to do about it?"

"Can you go down to his room and see if he's there?" Ted asked.

I sat up in the bed, closing my eyes and pushing the aether under my door. It danced along the hallway, down the stairs, curling past the demons arguing about the *Golden Girls*. From there, the aether continued through the darkened space before pausing in front of Luke's door. I took a breath. *I don't want to catch him again.* The aether pulsed, sending back nothing. His familiar energy wasn't there. I let the aether slither under the door to find an empty room.

"He's not there," I said out loud.

"What," Ted shouted. "You haven't left your room."

"I don't need to. Trust me, his room is empty."

"Whatever, I've had this bad feeling since I woke this morning that something was wrong. Do you know who he was on patrol with last night?"

"Not really. It can't be too hard to figure out. I had the night off."

"I went out for a few hours, but not with him."

"Then that means that Kaity and Luke should have been on patrol."

"I already checked with Kaity. Apparently, she didn't go out last night even though she was supposed to. I'm calling a meeting in an hour. Something bad has happened." He hung up.

Ted's voice sent a shiver down my spine.

If Luke and Kaity didn't go, then that left Grace and Chris. Grace actually going on a patrol was highly unlikely. That left Chris.

Chris.

Chris.

Christo!

I yelled, trying to project my thoughts to him. While he could communicate with me from a farther distance, sometimes my messages wouldn't connect. He kept saying that, in time, the connection would grow stronger as our bond grew, but I had to wonder if I truly wanted that. I was still resentful that he hadn't asked my permission before bonding us together.

Shaking it off, I grabbed my jeans from yesterday and

a sweater out of the duffel I had dragged from my father's house.

Coming out of the bathroom, I ran into Chris. Of course, he'd heard me and decided a visit would be a better response.

"So, you're not happy to see me?" he said, settling into one of the chairs.

"It's not like that," I said, trying to lighten the mood. "Luke is missing."

He tilted his head.

"No one has seen him since yesterday. He didn't come back in from patrol last night," I said, prompting a response from Chris.

"We parted ways after midnight. He said he wanted to check out some of those vampire nests."

"So, you left him to do that alone?"

Chris stood up and stalked over, peering down at me. "I was due back for my tests, and he didn't want my company anymore. There's only so much I can do to get your friends to like me."

Backing up a few steps, I eyed Chris. "I know, I'm sorry. They're calling a meeting soon. Can you come?"

He nodded, and we headed to the cafeteria.

The shouting started two minutes into the meeting. Ted and Kaity nearly drowned out Christo's calm, reasonable explanation.

"Guys," I spoke during a brief pause in their triad. "Can we stop yelling and talk in regular voices? We need a plan of action. Not a system of blame. Luke's an adult and has been doing this for several years. We're all aware of the risks."

"Ember's right. We need a plan of action," Grace said, looking at Ted, who finally sat down across from us.

"Yes, you're right." Ted's voice lowered. "Since we can all be out in daylight, we should split into teams and search the grids."

"Sound plan. I have a business meeting. I'll check back later," Chris said before disappearing.

Nice, real nice, Chris.

Be safe.

I shrugged, turning to Grace. "Are you able to help?" I couldn't remember if she was working or not.

"Yes, I already called in and told them I lost my cat."

I raised an eyebrow at her. "Luke's not a cat."

"I know that, Ember, but what else was I going to say?" She tilted her head and spoke in a higher octave. "Sorry, Mr. Peters, I can't come in today because one of my vampire friends is missing. I need to go look for him." She gave me a pointed look. "He would have called the police and wanted to help look."

I shook my head as Ted and Kaity took off. Bob, Scout, and Chase headed into the tunnels in case Luke had gone down there away from the sun. I waited for Grace before we headed out also.

"Let's start at the edge of town and work back toward the school," Grace said, putting the car in reverse.

I nodded, and she sped off before I clicked my seat belt in place. We parked a few blocks outside the suburbs on the west end. Walking back into town, we searched the area twice before doubling back to get Grace's car.

We stopped at Eats! for lunch after the unproductive morning of searching. Ted had called to say he hadn't found anything either. *Would we find anything?* In the four hours of our searching, no word had come from Luke. While Ted could trace cell phones through his mad hacker skills, nothing was turning up, which meant Luke's phone was probably dead. *Please, let it only be his phone.*

I shook my head away from the thought. Grace had wanted to continue searching and forgo lunch, but I needed sustenance to continue since I'd missed breakfast.

"Where could he be?" Grace muttered. She picked up her sandwich and took a huge bite, looking at me as she talked and chewed. "Hurry, eat."

I nodded, not wanting to argue with her. She was just as worried as I was about her cousin. If he had gone looking into those nests and gotten caught . . .

We need to find him.

"Do you know if Ted found Luke's map of the nests?" I asked, pulling the bacon off my sandwich and eating it first.

"He's checked at the school, but he's already called Chris to get another map."

Finally, Ted had a good idea instead of blaming people like he did this morning. Maybe we would find Luke by tonight.

Loud voices from the other side of the café caught my attention—the redhead Grace had snagged the date with.

Why didn't she seem more interested? She practically drooled the last time he'd been in here.

"So, how did your date go the other night?"

"Last night," she said and shrugged. "He wasn't as nice a guy as I thought he was."

"Oh."

Grace finished and stood up, and I shoved the last remaining piece of my sandwich in my mouth, following her. Throwing my trash away, I watched the redhead surrounded by his friends. They all laughed at something while they eyed Grace. *Are all men jerks?*

Grace opened the door to leave, and I sent a wave of wind toward the boy, knocking his chair out from under him. He jumped to his feet with a confused expression.

Once outside, we walked around the corner of the building before Grace giggled. "Did you see that?" She twisted her head and laughed. "He was such a jerk last night, even indicating that I made more money than him, so I should pay."

I frowned. "Asshole."

>———>

After pulling into the school parking lot with the morning light rising behind us, I thanked Grace for the ride and headed inside. I gasped. I'd forgotten the meeting with Dad. *Shit.*

And shit didn't even cover it. While I wouldn't have been able to shoot with him and more than likely had to admit my bow got destroyed, at least we could have talked.

Shutting the door to my room, I really only wanted to sink into my covers and take a nap before I needed to be ready for work in four hours. But in Dad's eyes, calling him now would be a much better scenario for me than if I were to do it later today.

I laid my phone down on the table as I took off my clothes and tossed them onto the chair across the room. I hit his contact and waited. *Will it go through, or will it roll to voicemail?*

"Hello."

Pausing from unhooking my bra, I spoke toward the phone. "Hey, Dad."

"Emma," he said.

Yep, he was not taking any shit today.

"Sorry about last night." I stopped my mouth from moving. *Did he really want to know why I missed, or would it be better to keep the real reason from him?* Closing my eyes, I decided the truth was the best way. "Something important came up with Luke that I needed to take care of."

"I see. Supernaturals, then."

His comment was more offensive than I expected. I threw my bra to the floor, looking around for my robe.

The robe slid over my shoulders. I yelped and jumped forward, spinning around, ready to attack whoever was in my room.

Christo stood smiling in my direction, obviously liking what he saw.

"Em?" Dad's voice rose with concern.

"Sorry, Dad," I said, turning back around to pick up my robe from the floor. Putting my arms through the sleeves, I muttered, "It's just Chris."

"Chris?" he questioned.

"Hello, Mr. Ellington," Chris said in the background, a smile playing on his lips.

Fuck, what did I just do? I plopped down in a chair.

"Hello, who are you?"

"My boyfriend, Dad."

"Boyfriend." I could hear my dad grind his teeth over the line. "I thought you were seeing Luke again."

Glancing back at Chris, I saw his body tense. *Why are they both concerned about me dating Luke?* "No, Luke is with Kaity." *I think.* "I've been seeing Chris for a couple of months now."

"Why have I never met him?"

Maybe because you're not talking to me.

"He helps run his family's business in Canada and isn't here that often," I said.

"I'll need to meet him. I've got business out of town the rest of this month. How about the second Wednesday for dinner."

Surprised at the eagerness in his voice, I agreed. The line went dead, and I turned to look at Chris lounging on the other chair.

"Find him?" he asked.

I shook my head and walked over to him, close enough that he pulled me into his lap.

"You will." He nuzzled my neck. "I have faith in you,

Queen. Where could the vampire boy have disappeared to anyway?"

"I hope so. We were out all night."

He carried me to bed. "Then sleep. I'll be back later tonight to help with the search."

He disappeared.

Chris helping would hopefully get better results than today. *What happened to Luke?* Kaity's eyes had been puffy and bright red this morning. She'd asked Ted if he thought Luke would leave them all. *Why would he leave?*

I knew he wouldn't and repeated it to Kaity. That only seemed to make her cry more. She clung to my shirt for almost an hour before Ted talked her into going home for some rest. I closed my eyes. *I'll find him. He's got to be here somewhere. He would have told me before he left.*

Sixteen

LUKE

The cold seeped into my body from the cement wall I was chained to, reminding me I was still alive. I didn't know how many days I had hung in the darkness of this crypt. The putrid smell of death lingered in the stagnant air. My arms were held out from my sides while my feet were spread and chained at the base of the wall. *Could I still be saved? Would they notice I'm missing?*

My tormentor stood before me with a smile on his lips.

"Brother, there is no need to suffer," he said for the millionth time since I'd been ambushed at the vampire nest in the old hospital. "You should be honored that I'm giving you this choice."

I spit the blood dripping down my face onto the dusty floor. "Honor? That's a new one. You have none."

His smile widened. Nothing seemed to faze him.

"I've not always given you a choice," he said.

Like I knew what he was talking about.

"There were times that my anger got the best of me."

"You're talking to the wind," I muttered, closing my eyes for a brief moment.

He was closer when I opened them.

"I'll be back later tonight with a treat for you. I can see you need one."

A treat? What could the bastard be planning now? My arms and legs had been stretched, pinned to the wall for far too long. I'd lost all feeling. Since the day I'd awoken here, Rabon's vicious attacks had not produced the answer he was looking for.

Apparently, "no" wasn't the correct answer. *Go figure.*

Rabon sneered back at me before stepping out of the crypt.

Please just leave the damn door open.

"Are you sure, brother? You'll have to make the choice."

I sneered at the question. The same question he'd asked every day. I leered at him, knowing the end would be near and it would most definitely piss him off.

"No. *Brother.*"

He left, giving me ample time to wonder what everyone was doing. Ted worked as a computer software developer for an online company during whatever hours he saw fit. The other amount of time was spent researching information about Rabon or hunting down vampires. There was nothing he could have done differently to save Nathan. It wasn't his fault. *I should have told him.*

The last few weeks, I could see the difference—bags under his eyes, his belt notched tighter, and he was withdrawn into himself. Beating himself up each day wouldn't make Nathan happy. He would want him to move on.

I'm sure Kaity was still upset with me, but maybe she'd be worried. I didn't want to dwell on the pain in my heart when I remembered how she looked at me that day. I'd been an ass. *Fuck me.*

I'd bet my life on Ember with the short amount I had left. She was the only sane one out of the bunch despite everything going on in her life. If anyone could find me, it would be her.

Seventeen

EMBER

"Jump, dance. Let's make sweet love tonight." My sassy ringtone interrupted the silence of the bank. I accidentally knocked it across my station instead of grabbing it.

"Phone off, Em," Denise said beside me.

I nodded, bringing my phone up to switch it to silent. *I need to change that.* Eyeing the notification on the screen, I saw it was from Kaity.

Turning the screen black on the message, I assisted the next person in line, wondering what Kaity sent me. She wasn't handling Luke's absence well. It had been weeks since we last saw him. We were all worried that Luke may have met his fate. Kaity most of all.

Once my shift ended, I read her message. She wanted to talk without the others and wondered if I'd pair up with her tonight. I agreed.

Ted came into the school every morning to do his research on vampire nests. We destroyed the ones that

Luke had been looking into but hadn't found a lead until the old hospital. Luke's phone had been found under an old mattress. Ted hacked into the phone by remembering Luke's mom's birthday.

I drove back to the school and rushed in as Christo was due to arrive any minute to pick me up. *How will Dad react to Chris?* I wasn't sure I wanted to know, but the inevitable hour was upon me. I grabbed my navy blue dress that hung on the makeshift curtain I'd installed. After changing, I checked my makeup and hair again, but as I lifted the hair straightener, the aether tingled with his essence. I turned the straightener off instead and ran a brush through it.

"Are you ready?" he called through the door.

I stepped out of the bathroom, and he wrapped his arms around my waist.

"Didn't you bring a car?" I asked as the room shifted.

We landed in the darkness of the restaurant's back parking lot.

"Whoa, buddy, you can't just pop around whenever you feel like it. What if someone saw us?" I snapped before stepping through the overgrown grass connecting to the sidewalk.

He pulled me to a stop, wrapping his arms around me again, tightening me into his warm embrace. "It's going to be okay," he whispered.

My eyes watered. "You can't know that."

He laughed, shaking me as he said, "Your dad will love me. Everything will be fine."

He gave me another squeeze before kissing the top of

my head and interlocking our hands as we headed toward the front of the restaurant.

I slowed down. A line of people was waiting inside the steakhouse.

Christo leaned down and whispered, "Trust me."

I smiled and nodded. I just needed Dad to forgive me. This distance between us hurt, but I knew I had hurt him.

"Remember, no powers."

Chris rolled his eyes but pulled me through the crowd inside the building. I doubted we would be seated anytime soon, so my mouth hung open as we were escorted back to an open table.

"How?" I said, glancing back at the long line. "There's a million people in here."

He pulled the chair out for me, and I sat.

Chris smiled, taking the seat to the right of me. "I called ahead."

When did he have time to call ahead? He had sent me a message earlier saying he might run late because of his trials.

"How did your tests go today?"

He laid his hand over mine. "It went well. I hope you haven't forgotten about the gala and needing a dress?"

Of course I'd forgotten. Between Luke missing, too little sleep, and then worrying about Dad, I couldn't keep anything straight.

He shook his head. "If you need money to buy one, just ask, Ember." He leaned closer, his warm breath against my ear, and whispered, "What I have is yours now."

"Em," a voice I knew well called out.

I broke away from Chris, brushing invisible dirt off my dress as I stood to hug my father. Wanting it to mean so much, I tightened my hold on my dad, then released him. He hadn't hugged me back. Chris stood up, placing his hand on my back, giving me a small squeeze as he held the other out to my dad.

"Chris Greyson. It's great to finally meet you, sir."

"Heath Ellington, nice to meet you."

We sat down as the server came by to take our drink orders. When she left, I tried to think of something to say, but this place was a bit too public to talk about our supernatural problems.

"Um, how have you been?" I asked as Chris's hand slid into mine under the table. *Why is this so hard?* "I'm sorry," I blurted.

He stiffened at the words, then gave a short nod.

I didn't get the feeling he was forgiving me that easily. The sounds of the restaurant came back into focus as the server put down our drinks and asked for our orders. Of course, none of us had reviewed the menu, so we buried our heads.

After we gave the server our orders, Dad asked, "Chris, what type of business does your family run?"

I gave Chris a slanted look, curious to hear what he'd say. He smiled at me before turning back to my father.

"We've been in business a long time, mostly investing in stocks and other platforms. My father passed away ten years ago, and my grandmother has finally told me it's my time to take over. So, I've been learning about the day-to-day aspects of the business from her and the other board members."

"And Emma said you live in Canada?"

Christo bumped my shoulder lightly before turning back to my dad. "Ah, well, my family owns quite a few houses around the world. My favorite is in British Columbia. Which is where I stay when I'm not in Happy Valley."

"Really, I've never traveled outside the States. Are you Canadian?"

He was hiding something, and while I never enjoyed having that smile pointed at me, it was probably best for my dad. Again, I watched Chris smile, the smile I knew too well.

"I'm American. The business is headquartered in New York, and I grew up there. I'll have to fly there in a month for a benefit dinner."

My father nodded, and conversation flowed between him and Chris. I sat back in my chair, watching their facial expressions as they learned of their common interests. My father actually seemed to like Chris.

During my entire relationship with Luke, Dad had been adamant he wasn't the one for me. That I shouldn't have "narrowed my playing field." *His words, not mine.* At the time, we were so infatuated and even continued in secret when he wouldn't let us meet.

His name is in your thoughts again.

Christo's voice floated through my head, and I turned

to look at him. He had to know I didn't still have those feelings for Luke. Wasn't that there in my thoughts?

But do you love me?

Gasping at the intruding question, I sloshed the water I had picked up, and it landed on my dress.

"Shoot," I muttered, setting the glass down before I ended up pouring the whole thing on myself.

I grabbed the napkin Chris handed me and sighed at his smirk.

After dabbing most of the water off my lap, I laid the napkin on the table, assuring my father I was okay. That nothing was wrong. The glass just slipped. I sat with my hands in my lap on top of the wet spot, wishing it was dry when the tiniest tickle brushed my hand.

I jerked in my chair.

Dad scrutinized me, raising his eyebrow.

"Sorry, hiccup," I muttered.

I gritted my teeth, hoping not to make a scene in front of my dad.

I didn't know how to stop, so I let the energy flow through me. I watched the water rise up from the dress. I peeked at my dad, but he was in a conversation with Christo about football. He hadn't noticed the floating water droplets. Closing my eyes, I finished the process. The dress was dry again.

Opening my eyes, I saw the look Chris gave me and knew he would tease me later tonight. Looking around the building at all the families chatting happily, I doubted anyone had spotted me. But the server appeared seconds later. It had been stupid on my part. An additional headache I wasn't prepared for.

We took a few minutes to eat in silence, during which my phone buzzed, reminding me I had put it on vibrate. I read the message from Ted.

There is still no sign of Luke.

I sighed before putting my phone face down on the table.

Could he survive this long without blood? Or was he somewhere he had access to it? Picking up a piece of popcorn shrimp, I realized I'd never seen Luke actually drink blood. At least he hadn't at the bar. But he did have a mini fridge in his room, so maybe he drank it there.

Chris's phone started to ring, and he quietly excused himself to answer the call.

"Em," Dad started, putting down his fork. "I know you wanted to talk, and this isn't really the place. Chris says he can shoot, so how about tomorrow morning we meet at the range?" But before I could answer, he continued, "Chris seems like a nice, normal guy. I'm really looking forward to getting to know him."

My smile froze on my face. *Normal.* "That would be nice."

He nodded and continued to eat. His eyes were warmer now, not as cold and distant as they had been. *Would it be different if he knew Christo is an Immortal demon?* More than likely, but until I needed to tell him that, I wouldn't.

And I was getting up in the morning to shoot even though I was meeting Kaity to patrol tonight. I had to do it. This talk needed to happen. I knew he could see how I felt. *He has to accept me.* Smiling, I plucked another shrimp off my plate.

Chris came back, and I leaned over and whispered, "Everything okay?"

He leaned into me, giving my forehead a light kiss. "Yes."

I sighed at the contact and turned back around in my seat. Dad sat wide-eyed, watching our little exchange. I blushed. He smiled before he took a drink.

As the server took away the dishes, Chris asked, "Mr. Ellington, do you want to join me at the bar for a drink?"

Dad darted his eyes down to the watch he always wore. "I think one drink would be fine." He turned to me. "Em?"

I hesitated. It was already later than I thought it would be with the restaurant being so crowded. "I need to get going."

Chris stood, helping me out of my chair. "Let me walk you out."

Dad nodded, and again, his eyes sharpened.

I walked beside Chris as we headed back around the building, his hand interlaced with mine. When we were far enough away, he wrapped his arms around me, bringing me in close as he lowered his head to my lips. When I opened my eyes again, we were back at the school.

"Be safe," he whispered in my ear before he disappeared.

Eighteen

EMBER

I rushed to my room to grab the pair of leggings I had set out earlier. I changed from the dress into a long-sleeve, baggy shirt and bent down to tie my tennis shoes. Once I pulled my hair back into a ponytail, I jogged across town to the courthouse where I was to meet Kaity. It was only a few blocks from the school, but after drinking a little at the restaurant, I didn't want to drive.

"Hey, Kaity," I said, coming to stand on one side of her.

She jumped and then laughed off her fright.

"Are you ready?"

She nodded and stepped down to walk with me. I wasn't sure where to look. We had all combed the grid several times.

"What if we don't find him?" she asked quietly as we made our way through the back alley behind the gym Luke used to teach boxing to grade school kids.

She slowed down, waiting for my answer.

I pulled her to a stop under the one lamp in the alley. "You can't think like that. He's strong. He will be okay."

She nodded again, looking at the exit door. "I first met Luke here for a boxing class." She giggled. "I didn't know it was a children's class, but he asked me to stay anyway."

I noticed she went silent again, and I turned to look at her.

"I was so mad at him that day before he went missing," she said, pausing again. "I thought we were magic together."

"You will see him again," I said, patting her shoulder.

Tears began streaming down her face. "But he doesn't want to see me. I thought that day—that day you interrupted us. I thought it meant we were finally getting back together. He thinks because he's a vampire that we shouldn't be. But I love him so much." She hiccuped.

Pushing her red hair out of her face, I listened as she cried from her broken heart. "Maybe he will change his mind."

We stood there for some time, and I yawned again. Neither of us was up to searching tonight. Kaity needed to go home. We both needed the rest and to try again another night.

"Let's go home." I pulled Kaity down the alley, gently pushing her toward her house.

"But we haven't searched anywhere."

"It's already really late, and you aren't in any condition to fight vampires."

She nodded, and we walked along back toward the courthouse where she'd parked.

Kaity climbed into her car and tilted her face up to me. Her eyes were just as red as her hair. "Thank you, Ember. Are you walking back to the school?"

I nodded.

"Are you going through the graveyard? I know it's much quicker, but it's so creepy with the guy on the horse."

I laughed, "It's not that bad."

Kaity nodded and closed her door before driving off.

That statue *was* beautifully creepy. I swore the eyes followed me.

A sudden coldness seeped into my bones as I walked through the gates of the oldest graveyard in Happy Valley. My thin leggings and T-shirt seemed logical to kick vampire ass, but now, with the wind kicking up the end of my shirt, I wished I had worn something heavier.

I passed the statue and ventured to my favorite place in Happy Valley, wandering through the tombstones. *Will tomorrow give me what I need to move on with my life?*

I made it to my spot but stared at the pile of rubble. Tears welled in my eyes as I surveyed the damage. *Who the hell did this?* The fountain bowl was shattered into tiny pieces, wood splinters sticking out of the dirt, and only weeds were left where the flowers once grew.

"It's okay, dear."

I frowned up at Gran, a small smile on her face as she

stood behind the ruined tombstone. Beside her was a face I missed.

My words caught in my throat. "Nathan," I whispered.

Nineteen

EMBER

Nathan smiled. "Hey, Em."

"But how?" I asked, stepping around the rubble. I tried to touch him, but my hand drifted through.

He shrugged. "She said she needed help to explain and asked if I wanted to venture beyond the veil."

"I'm so sorry." I hiccuped. "I'm sorry I couldn't save you."

"It's not your fault, Ember. I knew what I was getting into."

I wiped the tears from my face and turned back to Gran. "That means . . ." I paused, fighting the tears once more. "That you're gone too."

Nathan turned to look at something behind them. "I gotta get going. Make sure Ted moves forward. He can't live in the past. Also, tell everyone Luke is alive, and he's . . ." With his last words, he faded into nothingness.

He's where? He's alive, thank god.

Gran stepped closer to me and cupped my cheek, but

there was no contact. Warmth spread over my cheek as if she had.

"I built this for you." She swept her hand down at the ruins.

"For me?"

"A place where we could come to pay tribute to your mother. Don't worry, it can be rebuilt. Your mother is buried at Anu as are all of our ancestors. Unfortunately, this small space is just for you. But I didn't have time to show you before I died."

Tears leaked down my face. *Mom could visit me like Gran.* Maybe someday I could meet her and know if I resembled her.

"Be strong, child. I came to warn you—"

"Are you okay?"

I tensed at the strong male voice, wiping fiercely at the wetness on my cheeks. Gran and I looked at the same time. Kit's lean body stood behind the bench.

Gran whispered as she disappeared, but my mind didn't register her words.

"Do you often talk to yourself?" he asked, stepping closer and glancing down at the tombstone.

My fists tightened at my sides. "Did you do this?"

He halted, locking eyes with me. "Why would I?"

"Why wouldn't you? You attacked me," I snapped. "You're not who I thought you were."

I raised my fist, engulfing it in flames.

He crossed his arms. "Who did you think I was?"

The question made me pause. *Jerk. Asshat. A friend.*

I released the fire back to the world as I answered him. "Just a regular guy."

He laughed, stepping closer, not seeming to be afraid of me despite my show of power.

"Who are you?"

"Kit," he said, a foot from me. "I thought we'd already established that."

I rolled my eyes. "Why did you attack me before?"

His eyes seemed to soften. "I'm sorry." He ran his hand over his scruff. "I was tracking someone else."

"Tracking? Who?"

"A demon."

Christo.

"Why?" I asked.

He lifted an eyebrow. "Demons are evil. Do you know where I can find it?"

In my bed tonight.

I took a step back. "No."

Kit stepped closer, his face inches from mine. "You're lying."

"Leave," I breathed.

Shock washed over his face before he masked it. He stood still a minute longer before backing away.

He half turned, calling over his shoulder, "Next time I may not spare you."

"I don't intend to," said a distance voice in the shadows.

Twenty

KIT

I tensed as shadows moved around us. Vampires stalked in a circle, just far enough away that there was no clear escape. There were at least twenty. Nests weren't usually this big. *Where did they all come from?*

I pulled back my jacket, gaining access to my throwing stakes. "This won't end well for you," I said to them.

They hissed at us.

I extracted a smooth wooden blade from its slot, and with a flick of my wrist, I aimed and released one after another, clearing the first wave of balaur.

Ember swung around, palms ignited. She blasted the closest vampire to her, leaving nothing behind except ash. She ducked away from a claw swiping toward her face, then sent back a flaming fist into his heart. Ashes flew over me, coating my dark uniform and distorting my vision, sending me into a coughing fit.

Balancing the wooden blade between my fingers, I

sent it flying through another dead heart. I dodged the next one coming for my throat. Another vampire grabbed my arm, knocking me off balance. I fell against Ember. *Crap.* She lost her balance, and we tumbled to the ground. I spun to break her fall, avoiding a headstone.

I squinted up to see another vampire poised to attack again.

Keeping my arms wrapped tightly around Ember, I rolled us away from the assault and dislodged the vampire from my arm, her scent of the first spring rains enveloping me as we tumbled. She clung to my shoulders until we came to a stop.

I stood, heaving Ember up to her feet. She swayed against me, and I pulled her out of the way, retrieving my knife and slicing through the vampire's throat. He backed away a few paces, clinging to his throat.

I turned my attention back to Ember. "Are you okay?"

She nodded, and her eyes narrowed as flames lit up her fingers.

Good. I turned back to my assailant and thrust my weapon into its heart. More ash flew into the air.

"Stay standing, or you're going to get us killed."

"Thanks," Ember started, "but I don't need your help. You can actually leave. I do this all the time."

I turned, giving her my back, and positioned my arms, ready for the next wave.

Ember pivoted, bringing forth several fireballs floating in the air before flinging them across the tombstones. We worked together for several minutes, back to back, as the vampires attacked. Their numbers seemed endless.

"Where are they coming from?"

"I don't know," Ember said behind me. "I thought the park was their favorite hangout."

I've only seen this many together one other time.

Ember held her arms up, aiming for the next attacker, but an unseen force sent her flying to the ground.

What the hell was that?

I cast a glance over to her. She seemed to be okay, but a swarm of beasts was headed for her. I killed the one before me when a blow to my chest sent me over a tombstone. Landing by her, I struck again and again, keeping the beasts from tearing her to pieces, but there were more coming.

"Get up!" I yelled at her as I scrambled to my feet, pulling her along with me.

Ember stabilized herself, her fist engulfed in flames. She stepped up to my side.

"We need to get out of here. There are too many," I said.

Ember nodded in agreement, but there wasn't a clear escape route. She took a step away from me and closed her eyes. The moment she opened them, flames leaped from the ground, encasing each balaur.

I watched them burn alive. *So much power.*

A minute passed before the screams died out.

"Neat trick," I said, turning to her. "But you missed one." I nodded toward the one I'd seen fleeing.

She glanced in that direction. A lone vampire was half sprinting, half limping away from us. She switched up her stance and held her arms out as if she were holding a bow. She summoned her flames in the shape of an arrow and released it. It soared through the air until it started its decline, impaling the vampire before it reached the cemetery gates.

Ember turned to me with a smirk. "Satisfied?"

More than you know. I crossed my arms at the intruding thought.

She collapsed to her knees.

"Are you okay?"

She nodded, and I helped her to her feet. Our eyes locked, and I was held in place by the same violet eyes I'd been entranced by before.

An owl hooted in the distance, and Ember stepped away from me, her own eyes wide with recognition of something I couldn't name.

"Good work. I can see our fight will be interesting." I headed out of the graveyard, picking my wood blades up off the ground as I went.

At the front gate of the cemetery, a chill swept down my spine—the memory of our conversation before we were attacked slipping back in. *Ember was lying.* I could see it in her stance, the constriction of her muscles. Her eyes had lit with recognition when I mentioned the demon. She knew who I was hunting. *But why would she protect a demon assassin?*

I stopped at the gate, glancing behind me one last time. There would be time to track her later. She would definitely lead me to my target. *This assignment will finally be over.* A sigh escaped my lips.

I tensed at the scent of the first spring rain on the air that swept in with the fog. *Ember.* My body registered something. I started back into the graveyard. Scanning the area, I walked faster and faster until I was sprinting. Finally, I stood at the broken memorial. I swept my gaze over the thick fog, but she was no longer there.

I must have imagined it.

I turned again to head out, but something crunched beneath my boot. I bent down to pick up the phone. Spider cracks were spread across the screen. *Broken. She wouldn't have left this. What happened?*

I took another look at my surroundings, finding indents of shoe prints, but there were only two. I traced our last steps during the vampire fight. Vampires didn't make prints because of the density of their bodies, but they left other indicators—like flaky dead skin lying on the well-kept lawn. There were two additional sets of footprints on the other side of the memorial. One small and lighter than the other person.

Coming around the monument, I knelt down, plucking one silver strand of hair from the blades of grass. I pulled out a small, clear plastic bag and secured the DNA. It was highly doubtful that whoever owned this hair was in any normal databases, but the Cross was developing a new program to manage balaur information.

I backtracked through the area, carefully scanning my surroundings, but forty-five minutes later, I ended back where I had started. *Nothing.* No trail to follow. The prints just ended after walking between headstones.

Ember had vanished.

My phone vibrated in my pocket, and I answered immediately.

"Yes?"

I listened to the instructions. Nodding, I hung up. I was out of time. Despite coming this close to finding the demon assassin, I was being recalled to Berkeley. I had fourteen hours until check-in and was reported as MIA.

"Shit," I whispered. I placed Ember's phone down on the broken monument.

I have one more hour.

Twenty-one

EMBER

Rubbing my temples, I opened my eyes to darkness. My body throbbed. The room smelled of musty decay. In the graveyard, I had been stopped dead by a woman standing in my path. She was gray. Her hair, her eyes, and even the clothes she wore.

Her gray gloved hand had come up, and she'd snapped her fingers in my face. Heaviness had come over me. I'd blinked several times, but an unwavering sleepiness hit me. My limbs had become like lead. I tried to shake the sudden fog from my head when it turned to black.

I crossed my arms as it was slightly cooler here than it had been outside. The only light filtered through the small windows and cracks at the top of the walls. I was in some sort of basement. Something crawled over my ankles, and I jumped to my feet, scanning my surroundings. A mouse ran off and disappeared into the darkness. My clothes were coated with mud.

"That's my favorite shirt." *I'll never get that out.*

A groan came from the far side of the room where light didn't reach. Pushing the aether into the space, I crept forward as my powers wavered. *Shit, I'm still too weak.* Gasping from the familiar energy, I rushed across the room, tripping and landing hard on my knees. My leggings ripped, and I could feel the blood dripping down my leg.

"Luke," I whispered, pushing myself up from the ground.

I created a ball of fire, lifting my hand. The orb floated in front of me. After my eyes adjusted, I took tiny shuffling steps. I stepped around the coffin in the middle of the room, pausing to glance around again. *This is a crypt. Am I in one of the dozens that are on the west side of the cemetery?*

One of my closest friends hung from the wall.

"Luke," I uttered.

He didn't budge at the sound of his name. *He's too pale to be alive.*

I stepped closer, rising to my tiptoes, and placed my hand on his cheek. His skin was cold to the touch. He took a labored breath, and I breathed a sigh of relief. His wrists and ankles were shackled by chains that looped through rings attached to the wall.

"Luke, talk to me. Are you okay?"

His eyes opened. Brown rimmed with red.

He lunged at me.

Shock rippled through me, and I stumbled back, trying to gain my balance. My foot caught against the broken floor, and I toppled again, scraping my palms on the debris. My fireball was shrinking with each breath.

"Our guest has awoken," someone said behind me.

My eyes widened in the darkness, trying to locate him. A match lit, and light shuddered against the walls, illuminating Rabon's deadly smirk. He flicked the match into a puddle, catching it on fire. It roared to life on the opposite wall, bathing the room.

Releasing what was left of my fire into the universe, I climbed to my feet, but Luke's chains clanked. I pivoted back against the other wall.

This isn't good.

"Nice of you to stop by. Sorry I interrupted your little tryst with the *Cross*. Istros was wondering where all his friends were."

Istros? I darted my gaze from the nightmare on my right to Luke on my left. *It couldn't be.*

"You're lying," I spat at Rabon.

Not true. I was the Zodian Warrior, destined to put a stop to the Chaos Brothers. If Luke was a part of that . . .

I shook my head. *No!*

"I see my brother failed to tell you his secrets. *My dear*, it is very much the truth." He walked across the room and grabbed Luke's chin, lifting it up. "Didn't you ever wonder why he was so different from other vampires?"

Luke jerked his head out of Rabon's grip. "Fuck you."

Rabon chuckled as he moved to stop in front of me, lowering his head to mine.

I whispered, backing into the cold concrete behind me, "He's not like *you*."

"There's no use in fighting the truth."

I searched my powers again, but I'd used way too much trying to outdo Kit in the fight. And I still didn't know what that witch's spell had done.

"You sent the vampires."

He straightened. "Had to keep the *Cross* busy. But I didn't know you were out there too." He smiled. "I would have enjoyed personally taking care of you, but then I thought, 'What would my brother want?' He seems to care for you. It's evident since he fell to his death to save you."

How was I going to get us out of this one? Luke seemed deranged at best, dangerous at worst.

"What do you want?" My voice was barely above a whisper.

"Oh." Rabon leaned back against the crumbling coffin in the middle of the room, crossing his arms in front of him. "I told my guys to go out and find my brother a treat. You see," pointing at Luke, he continued, "he's been here a while and is a little dried out, if you know what I mean."

And I did know. Luke had been missing for almost a month now.

"Fortunately, you were at the wrong place at the wrong time." His smile grew. "What a bonus. When I learned my brother had lived despite jumping into the sea with the morning light in the sky, I didn't quite know that the girl he jumped for would also live." He took a decisive step toward me. "And now he'll do me a favor by getting rid of another Zodian."

If Rabon knew I was the Zodian Warrior, would he have killed me instantly? He planned to kill me anyway. I desperately wished the wall behind me would absorb me and take me to safety. But I knew my energy was too depleted.

When would the others realize I was missing and come looking? Would they be able to find us when they hadn't been successful in finding Luke so far?

Christo would notice I was gone, despite our connection not being very strong. He was my best hope. The others wouldn't be at the school until tomorrow morning.

Rabon took another step toward me. "I hope you enjoy your last hours with my brother. You'll be such a special treat when he awakes from his blood fever. Goodbye, my dear." He stepped away, heading back into the darkest corner of the crypt to throw words over his shoulder. "Hope you enjoy your meal, brother. You know where to find me when you change your mind." He chuckled, pulling open a door and walking out.

I sprinted toward it. The door closed before I got to it. I hadn't seen it when I first awoke. I pulled the handle, but it wouldn't reopen. I was too late. It was locked.

Turning, I looked at Luke, his body half-hidden by darkness. My gaze drifted to his blazing crimson eyes.

My eyes opened to everything bathed in red. There was another person in the room with me, but it wasn't Rabon, whose goons jumped me weeks ago. He'd gotten all of the covens of vampires and united them. The day I'd checked out the hospital, they'd been hiding out, waiting for me.

A familiar smell hit my nose. *She* was inches from me. Too close. She needed to move back before . . . My body lurched forward. She squeaked, and her heart rate spiked. I licked my dry lips. The tang of blood coated my nostrils, and I savored it, closing my eyes to cherish the aroma floating around me.

I yanked once more at the chains that held me. I'd woken in darkness and was weaker than I'd ever been since becoming a vampire. Rabon had explained that the chains were magically enchanted to take the victim's powers, basically turning them into a human. In my case, it brought out all the tendencies I'd been squashing for the last two years.

"Luke."

Her voice was soft, unlike that wretched bastard.

I groaned, but I didn't dare say anything. The roar of hunger filled my ears, fading out her voice. Demanding I feed the monster inside me. *The darkness.*

My son, you are no monster. You give me life with each act of destruction, and I cherish you.

Opening my eyes, I was no longer in that musty crypt but in a golden palace filled with artificial light. A man stood in front of me wearing robes of yellow silk. The room held an extravagant atmosphere while figures stood along the back wall, cloaked head to toe in white robes. Gold orbs hung from the ceiling, casting everything in a warm aura.

My followers, the man before me said.

Followers? Who was this guy? And how did I get here? Was this vision real like the other one?

Your body is breaking down. You must drink blood to sustain this life.

Typical vampires had to drink blood to sustain their existence, but I hadn't had to since the day I turned. What the hell was he talking about?

Forgive me, it's still early in your transition. Istros, I am Zamolxis, God of Darkness, God of the Underworld and Chaos. I granted your brother's wish in exchange for lifetimes of chaos the two of you will bring me. You were always the stronger of the two, but he was more trustworthy. You serve me. You were gifted this life and all those to follow.

"This isn't my life," I started, licking my dry lips.

You will remember your choices in time. Each time your body is reborn, the memories come back slower.

I closed my eyes; I could sense death was close. It had to be if I was having imaginary conversations with the God of Darkness. The god stood before me with a smug expression. If only I had the energy to pound it off his face.

Do what must be done to live today, for the rest of your days will bring me chaos.

The vision faded, and my eyes cleared to the world still doused in red.

Twenty-three

EMBER

After trying in vain to open the crypt's concrete door, I gave up. No wind or fire affected it. It was just too heavy for me to open and seemed to be magically sealed. I crossed over to the middle of the room, where the decades-old tomb sat. I hopped up onto the tomb, facing Luke. He started talking to himself, but otherwise seemed fine for the moment, but I wasn't about to move any closer.

The chains were attached to the wall he leaned against. His eyes opened and closed. He hadn't directed anything to me in the last twenty minutes, even though my wind had blown across his face. I really thought I could use the wind to push open the door. The only other option I had was to move the earth, but having never tried before, I was afraid I would collapse the building on top of us. And the longer I stayed in the crypt, the more fatigued I got.

After being here for an hour, a chill was settling in

my bones. The fire burning at the base of the wall was dimming with every breath. I summoned fire to my hands and breathed in the warmth, but it quickly dimmed.

That gray witch had done this.

"I'm out of ideas," I said to Luke. He didn't answer, so I continued, "I lost my phone when they captured me. Do you have yours?" I asked, hoping it would still be charged, though in the back of my mind, I remembered we'd found it at the old hospital.

He didn't answer me. His red eyes stared into my soul as I watched him.

What else could I do? My connection with Chris was blocked. A knot had formed in my stomach, getting worse each time I tried calling to him.

"Ember." Luke's voice was barely a whisper.

I jumped off the tomb and headed to him, making sure I was still out of reach. His eyes seemed clearer somehow.

"Luke, are you with me?"

He coughed. "Yeah, I feel so hungry."

"I know, but I don't have any food for you."

His eyes focused on my neck. "You're bleeding."

I knew my legs had been scratched when I'd fallen earlier, but I touched my neck and the stickiness on my collarbone. I jerked my hand down into the light. Blood covered my palm, and dizziness swiftly replaced the adrenaline I'd been operating on. *So much blood.*

Looking around for something to put against the wound, I saw some old white clothes in a pile. I crept closer and realized they weren't white clothes but bones.

Nope. I grabbed a part of my shirt and ripped a small piece off. I pressed it against the wound, hoping it would slow the bleeding.

"Luke, how are we going to get out here?"

He shook the chains. "Let me out!"

"I'm not sure that's a good idea."

"It's the only way. I've been watching for days. The door is heavy, but it's not locked."

"If it's not locked, then why can't I pull it open."

His eyes found mine in the darkness. "Ember, you're not even five and a half feet tall. And it's enchanted."

I narrowed my eyes, choosing to ignore his height comment for now. I went to stand before him. "I don't think letting you out is a good idea."

The chains clanked again. "It's the only way. I'm okay, really."

"You haven't had blood in weeks," I noted.

"I haven't had blood in two years," he corrected.

My eyes met his. "What?" *That can't be right. He turned two years ago.* "But don't you need blood every day to survive?"

He turned his head away from me. "I remember drinking blood that first morning—the morning of the accident. It's still hazy, but it was my father's blood. I'm sure of that now. I haven't needed it since, really. I've always been able to push down the impulse."

The horror of what he went through that early morning sank in. Drinking his father's blood after he was sure he had caused the accident that killed his parents.

"But you haven't had any blood since then?"

"No. Being locked away in these chains . . . They're filling my head with thirst. If you take them off, the need will go away." He paused, letting his words sink in. "Ember, there's no other way. I *can* open the door."

"But the blood," I repeated.

"As soon as I open the door, I'll take off, leaving you here. Safe."

Glancing around in the darkness of the tomb, I knew we wouldn't be getting out anytime soon unless I unlocked his chains.

Rattling made me tilt my head back to stare into his eyes. They were still rimmed with red, but more of his brown shone through. I trusted him.

I moved closer to inspect the metal. The wrist clamps were solid. It didn't look like there was a clasp that could release him. The loops holding the chains were attached to a plate embedded into the concrete. The easiest solution was to break those, and then he would at least be able to move around with the chains still on.

"Hold still," I said, taking a deep breath.

I summoned the energy to create fire in my palm.

I held my hand out toward the loop farthest from Luke, and the fire barely lit up the room. The eyelet heated slowly as the fire dimmed. I added more, focusing it into a single stream. There was no way I would be able to maintain the energy needed to melt the metal. I released the fire. The only option I had left was earth, but without practice, I could level the whole place. *Or we could stay here and die.* I closed my eyes, thinking back on all of Lyra's lessons and pinpointing the crucial piece.

Focus. Just like the single stream of flame, I could focus on only crumbling the stones behind the plate.

I cast my eyes around the room, finding a metal table meant for flowers. I moved it over to the wall and climbed up. Cupping my hands together around the plate, I sent energy through the stones. The vibrations slowly built. Dust soared down from the edges before chunks started cracking and falling at my feet.

"Luke, pull hard," I yelled.

Finally, it cracked, and I went to the other side and did the same thing. Soon the chain clattered to the floor, and I stepped back.

"Now you can open the door."

He looked down at his wrists, still shackled in the irons, and lifted his arms as if testing the weight of the metal. He raised his head, his eyes more red than before.

He lunged. Not at the door but at me.

I half turned, creating a fireball that extinguished against his chest. He caught my wrist, pulling it out and twisting it behind my back. His other arm wrapped around my stomach, bringing me tighter under his control. The chains clanked against the ground in tune with my pounding heart.

I cried out. "Luke, please stop."

Tightening his hold on my body, he lowered his mouth to the blood on my neck.

His fangs sank into my skin. Betrayal, fear, and all my trust flowed out with every drop he drank from me. I exhaled and invited the darkness in.

Twenty-four

LUKE

What is happening? The red in my vision dimmed, and darkness surrounded me. *Where am I?*

Ember?

Trying to break through the fog, I rubbed my eyes, but the smell of blood was so strong. My hands were drenched. The blood became more vibrant, and the room around me came into focus. I wasn't alone. And I wasn't in the crypt anymore.

I stood in a hall of sorts with stained-glass windows that allowed sunlight to shine through, making rainbows on the floor. Bodies lay strewn across the room—three high in some places. Screams could be heard from outside.

"In exchange, you will protect . . ."

I turned to the voice.

A woman knelt before me, her head turned down in respect. *Or is it fear?* She was dressed like th[e] ancient

Romans. Blood soaked her gown and sandals, pooling around her feet.

Where am I?

I refocused on the woman before me. She held out her right hand, wrist up toward me. I wasn't sure if I should grab it, but my hand reached out of its own accord. As our hands got closer, the light emitting from her wrist brightened.

Who is she?

Glancing around the room again, I didn't understand what I was being shown. Was it a memory? An omen of the future? Was this vision even real? The woman's hand was solid in mine.

My eyes fell on a body not far from where I stood. His face was turned toward me, eyes glazed over with death. Rabon. He lay in the pile of bodies.

This is weird. What was going on?

Movement brought me back to the woman at my feet. And my voice spoke without warning.

"My loyalty is yours."

It was then that she tilted her head up at me. *Ember?* Her face was so similar in that moment, but there were small differences the longer I gazed into her pale purple eyes. Ember's were more vivid, her skin darker. The woman before me smiled, and with a small nod, she released my hand. Flames engulfed her body. The fire started out orange but quickly turned bright blue.

Toward the end, it morphed into a violent shade of purple. The fire died before me, and in its place—pink and naked—lay a tiny baby girl with violet eyes.

Twenty-five

EMBER

I rolled over and stared into wide, blue eyes.

"Ember!" Grace shouted, jumping onto me.

She squeezed me as if she'd lost me.

"What happened?" I asked, rubbing my shoulder and wincing at the tenderness.

My eyes roamed around the room. *Parker Elementary.* Somehow I'd made it back to my room in the nurse's office. I pulled off the covers to see I was still wearing the crusty, ripped, and stained clothes I'd worn for patrol with Kaity.

Christo. The connection was back, but something wasn't quite right. Pain exploded in my head. I held the back of my head where the pain originated.

"Ember? Ember," Grace yelled. "I'll go get Luke."

She rushed out of the room.

"Luke's okay?" I cringed, gritting my teeth from the sharp ache.

Lying back onto the futon, I closed my eyes and sent

the aether out into the building to search for Christo. He was here, but I couldn't communicate with him. I could tell from their signatures that Grace was coming back with Ted instead of Luke.

"Ember, are you all right? Luke's been worried sick," Ted said, crossing the room to my bed.

"Is he okay?" I asked, keeping my eyes closed.

The bed dipped when he sat.

"Are you all right?" he said, touching my shoulder. "Did he take too much?"

"Too much?" *What was he talking about?*

"Luke had to drink your blood. He's sorry, but it's been getting to him that he could have killed you," he said softly.

Red eyes flashed behind my closed lids. I sat straight up in the bed, wide-eyed.

Grace steadied me.

"His eyes were red," I said. "They've been turning at different times over the last few weeks. I should have known something was wrong."

"He said as soon as he drank enough blood from you, his mind cleared. He realized what he'd done, whisked you out, and was heading to the hospital when . . ." He paused.

"When what?"

"How well do you know that demon?"

Chris? How did he play into this? He hadn't yet answered my thoughts. I pushed them out again, and pain intensified at the top of my spine. I bent forward, trying to relieve the pressure that seemed to build there.

"Ember, are you okay? What's wrong?" Ted stood from the bed. "I told Luke you still needed to go to the hospital. But he was too concerned with that demon."

"Where's Chris?" I asked.

Something was wrong with him. Though faint, I could feel it through our bond. The pain I was feeling wasn't mine. It was his. It was somehow transferring to me—a warning that he was in trouble. *I have to find him.*

I tried standing up, but the pain was too much, and my knees buckled and cracked against the floor. *God, if this is only a portion of his pain, what is happening to him?*

"Help me!" I gritted out.

Ted helped me stand, and we started out of the room. Grace followed us. Chris's presence started to grow closer.

"Where is he?" I demanded.

Ted stopped me. "Why does it matter so much?"

My fists clenched at my sides. "What's with all the secrecy? And why is everyone so focused on him?"

"After Luke escaped the crypt with you, he was stopped by Christo. Christo forced his blood down your throat, and before Luke could stop it, you'd swallowed it. They fought, but luckily for Luke, Kaity had been trying a location spell over and over again. She arrived at the right time and knocked Chris out with her magic."

"Why only Chris?"

Ted closed his eyes and took a deep breath like he was trying to calm himself.

"Tell me where he is. Now."

"In the gym," Ted said.

Grace wrapped her arm around my middle and helped me hobble down the hallway toward the gym. Every few seconds, there was a loud pop, like a firecracker, that reverberated through the halls.

Ted led the way, but before we entered, he faced me. "Kaity was able to get Luke out of the chains. She fixed them to use them on Chris until we figured out what was going on. He doesn't have access to his powers, so there's no need to worry."

"I never had anything to be worried about." I pushed open the door and stepped inside.

My mouth fell open at what was making the sound. Kaity was scrunched against the gym wall, her eyes close as if she was trying to hide from the horror of the room.

Luke pulled back the whip and swung at where Christo knelt at one end of the gym. It ripped through what remained of Chris's tattered shirt. He was chained securely to the floor and couldn't fight back. All he did was grimace, not making a sound.

"Stop!" Fatigue hit me, and I swayed.

Grace tightened her grip on me.

All eyes focused on me. But only one set of eyes held my interest. *Christo. He was worried.* "What are you doing, Luke?"

"He wouldn't answer our questions," Luke answered, standing stiffly several feet behind Christo.

Of course not. I asked him not to.

"We wanted to make sure his blood wouldn't turn

you into a half demon or something worse," Luke said, flicking the whip again.

He lifted his arm, tossing the whip behind him to gain speed, but his eyes were rimmed in red. Shoving away from Grace, I escaped her arms and rushed forward despite her pleas. I skidded between Christo and Luke, energy surging through me.

"Stop!" I started, but it was too late.

Luke's eyes widened, the red vanishing from sight. But his arm was in motion.

I held my place, knowing it would hurt. My body was too tired to summon any fire to protect us. At the last second, Christo rose up and tucked me under him. I lost my footing, landing on my ass.

Christo stared down at me. The blow hit.

"Are you crazy?" he whispered with a grimacing smile.

I touched his face. *This is my fault. I should have been honest with my friends.* "I'm sorry."

Luke dropped the whip and rushed over, clasping my arm and pulling me away from Christo. "Em, are you okay?"

Christo growled as I was dragged away from him.

Ted and Grace came up behind us and pulled me to my feet.

Grace's eyes locked onto mine. "What were you thinking?"

I'm the crazy one? Yes, Chris was a demon, and Grace's rant a few weeks ago made more sense. They all still feared demons. None of them could see that not all of them were bad.

"He's a friend. He's been helping us. Why would you do this?" I cried, clenching my fist.

Grace stepped forward. "He's not really *our* friend. We just want to make sure his blood won't harm you. As soon as he tells us the truth, he can go free."

I loved my best friend, but her words held no sincerity. There was no way around this situation except to reveal the truth. I should have done it weeks ago.

Just like with Dad, I was screwing up with my friends too.

"His blood heals me," I said finally, remembering what Christo had told me after he saved me all those months ago.

Those four words brought an end to the silence.

"Heals," Luke sputtered. "A demon's blood heals?"

"Yes, it does." *Because we're bonded.*

The others switched their gazes from me to Chris.

"Why would *he* heal you?" Grace asked finally.

"Because," I started and then sighed. "We're dating."

Grace stepped back as if I'd slapped her. Luke went rigid at my side.

"Dating?" they questioned in unison.

I looked at Kaity's face. She didn't seem as shocked as the others. *Could she have known?* "Yes, we've been dating for a while now."

"How did you get to know him that fast?" Luke asked.

"We already knew each other. I met him at college,

and we reacquainted ourselves when he came to Happy Valley with Jasmine and Sofia." I stepped closer to Christo. "Can someone undo these damn chains?"

"Why did you keep it from us?" Ted asked, going over to release Christo.

I helped Chris stand, touching him to make sure he was all right. His eyes sparkled. *Thank you for telling them.*

"Ember, why did you hide it?" Grace asked.

Not looking at her, I answered. "I wanted to keep it a secret because I didn't know if it would last, but then everything with my dad happened. It was all just too much." I turned to look at her. "I was going to tell you at our sleepover the other night, but you went off on that rant about how it was bad to allow the demons at the bar even though you don't know them. I didn't want to see the look you have on your face right now."

"I wouldn't have— I am not." Grace crossed her arms and huffed.

She squinted, and white light erupted around her.

"Kaity, can you take me home?" Ted asked.

Kaity nodded. She gave me a small smile before they vanished.

Luke stood in the same spot, his face impassive. When he caught my eyes, he said, "You should have told us. This could have all been avoided. I knew you were seeing someone, but I couldn't tell who."

He walked out of the room, leaving me with Christo.

"Are you all right?" I asked now that we were alone.

He nodded and pulled me close to him. "I'll heal.

What about you? I was so scared when I saw him carrying you out of the crypt like a corpse."

"You were in the graveyard?"

"Yeah. You called to me in your panic, but when I arrived, I couldn't find a trace of you anywhere. What happened?"

"You were right. Rabon happened," I said, steering Chris to a couple of chairs. "He was getting his revenge for the attack on his house."

"I'd hoped I wouldn't be right. Rabon's such a pain in the ass," he said.

I shook my head, refusing to revisit what I had learned about Istros. "How long was I out?"

"Long enough that we both missed early bow shooting with your dad."

"Great. I've already canceled on him the past two times. He's never going to forgive me."

We headed back to my room, and I pulled Chris down onto the futon before going to get the first aid kit. When I came back from the bathroom, he had pulled the remains of his shirt off.

You like what you see?

I smiled and motioned for him to turn around. With a damp cloth, I dabbed at the marks on his back, soaking up the dried blood. *How long was Luke whipping him?*

He twisted, grabbing my hands and yanking me into his chest. "This wasn't your fault."

"I'm sorry," I mumbled.

"Ember, don't worry. I heal quickly."

I pulled away. "Let me at least finish washing the blood away."

He nodded and gave me his back again, and I washed the last of the blood. Then I watched as the torn flesh fused together.

"Holy shit!" I yelped. His toned back glistened with sweat and blood.

He laughed. "I told you." He stood. "I, unfortunately, have to leave you for now."

Nodding, I let him go. He kissed my forehead before I snuggled into the covers to hide out for the rest of the day.

Fuck. How am I going to call Dad?

Twenty-six

EMBER

The next day, I came back from work using the front door instead of the normal side door in the hopes of not running into Grace. Christo had stopped by briefly this morning but told me that, with his final test approaching, he'd be busy the next few days.

I trudged down the hallway after a four-hour shift that felt like eight. I'd managed to purchase another phone, but Dad hadn't bothered to pick up my calls. Grace only answered to say she was busy and that she would call me back. I was zero for two.

Why can't they both just trust me? If only they could believe I would figure all this out on my own—that I could handle it myself.

I sat down and flung my tennis shoes off before lying down. My hand haphazardly half hung off the side of the futon, hitting a solid object. I jerked, rolling over, and saw my mother's box on the ground where I'd left it this morning. I'd been reading more of her journal.

Pulling the box onto the bed, I crossed my legs to get comfy as I pulled out the journal again.

I need to leave. I've heard rumors he's alive and my heart sings. I know it's the truth, but I don't understand why Heath would continue to lie to me. I must get to him as soon as possible, but Ember, my sweet girl. I don't want to reveal the truth of her birth. Once we leave Heath, we lose his protection.

I read the passage again. It was the last entry in the journal. It made no sense to me. Had Dad faked his own death? What had been going on those last few weeks when Mom was alive? This entry was dated two weeks before her death. Having been raised by my dad, it was clear she hadn't taken me with her. Was my mother's decision to leave me behind with Dad the reason I was alive?

What did she mean? The entire passage didn't make sense. She'd referenced "him" and "Heath" as if they were two different men. Had Mom been cheating on Dad?

I tossed the book onto the other side of the bed, bringing my head to my hands and resting my elbows on my knees. None of the contents of the box made sense—the receipt for the dress, the picture of my mother and her sister, and the knife. I'd been carrying the knife in my boots when I went out at night for extra measure and made sure to put it back into the box when I couldn't have it on me.

I pulled out the photo again, looking at the smiles on the girls' faces. They had to have been ten or so. They were happy. The background view was sandy, like a desert landscape, but it was hard to tell from the black-and-white photo.

I laid the photo back into the box and picked up the receipt for the dress. My mother had commissioned a very expensive dress and paid up-front. The receipt was stamped Paid. *What did my mother need a dress for?* The dress's description depicted a Kevlar corset, which I'd researched and found was military-grade bulletproof material, and the rest was flowing purple silk. *Why would my mother need a bulletproof dress?*

I fetched the new phone that had cost me half my savings and dialed the number on the paper. It rang several times and then rolled to voicemail.

"Hi, yes, I'm sorry . . . This may seem strange, but I have a receipt from twenty years ago for a dress my mother purchased from your boutique. I was wondering if you would have time to talk about it? You see, she died when I was very young, and I don't have many memories of her." I paused before reciting the information from the receipt and my number, and then I clicked End.

Jeez, I'm sure someone will call me back after that weird message.

I pulled my phone away from my ear when it started ringing and vibrating. I stared at the caller ID, noting it was the number I had just called. Hesitating to answer, I held the phone out in front of me.

What should I say? Crap.

Clicking the green answer button, I put the phone on speaker, setting it down on the bed in front of me since my hands were shaking. "Hello."

"You called about a dress we made?" an older lady asked.

"Um . . . not really about the dress."

"Oh, so you don't want it?"

The dress is still there? "I'm sorry, are you telling me the dress is still in the shop after twenty years?"

"Oh, yes, it was so gorgeous I couldn't give it away to just anyone. Kani was one of my best customers. I tried to get in touch with her mother, but the line never went through."

"You knew them?" I asked, hopefully.

The lady sighed on the other end of the call. "Yes, of course I knew them. Would you like to pick up the dress?"

I held in my squeal. "Yes, I want the dress!"

"Now, mind you, if you show up without the receipt and aren't who you say you are, I won't be able to give it to you, but if you are her daughter, then I think it would be wonderful for you to have it. You can pick it up on Friday, dear." The line went dead.

Friday? This week? That was in four days. I had to work, and it was a thirteen-hour drive. *How am I going to get there?* At least I was having better luck with this than calling Sofia. I'd tried her numbers several times over the last few days, but it kept rolling to a voicemail that had never been set up.

Twenty-seven

EMBER

I stood, stretching my legs, before walking down to get a celebratory bottle of wine from the cafeteria. Finding out my mother's dress was still at that shop and knowing I would soon have something from her life was awesome. It was a step in the right direction. I was finally going to be able to chat with someone who knew her. I dance-walked the rest of the way.

While the journals had given me some insight into her life, the dress seemed oddly significant. It was one of the better things to happen this week. Grace and Dad were still on the outs with me, and I had no idea what to do about that.

Walking into the cafeteria, I wasn't alone. *Istros.* Luke sat at the bar in the empty cafeteria. I honestly didn't know what time it was other than late.

I hesitated in the middle of the room.

"Join me," he called out.

I knew Luke wasn't mad like Grace was, but he was still a little put off by me dating Christo.

Sitting beside him, I saw that his injuries from being kidnapped had healed. Apparently, the amount of blood he drank from me in the crypt was enough.

He didn't say anything as I reached around the counter to grab a glass and then for the bottle he was silently nursing.

Pouring a small amount of whiskey, I kicked it back before I spoke. "How are you?"

His eyes darted to mine. "I'm healed if that's what you mean."

"You know I don't," I said, pouring myself a second drink and topping his glass off. "Really, how are you? Rabon had you for almost a month."

He tossed his drink before replying. "I can take a punch," he said with a smile.

I punched him in the shoulder and smiled as he tilted off his stool before he righted himself, rubbing his arm.

"Why didn't you tell me about Istros? When did you find out?"

He turned to me. "At the mansion. Rabon claimed I was his brother."

"Why didn't you tell any of us? Why didn't you tell me?"

"Why didn't you tell us about Christo?" he asked in turn.

I huffed. Of course he would turn it around on me. "I had planned to, but then you guys all seemed to hate him so much I thought I would wait, and well, it just got out of hand."

He smiled, tipping the bottle for another. "It's okay, but now more than ever, we should all be honest with each other."

"But there's still something you're not telling us. What else happened in the crypt? Why did Rabon kidnap you in the first place?"

"He wanted me to join him," Luke said, spilling half of my next round. He tossed it back and then added, "As his brother."

"But you're not Istros, right?" I took a sip, "This is good. What is it?"

Luke laughed, turning the bottle around. "Compliments of Rabon for surviving."

I read the note etched on the bottle. *You'll not get away so easily next time. Enjoy your final victory. Let the memories unfold.*

"He's unhinged," I uttered. "We need to tell everyone to watch their back. No more going out by ourselves, always in teams."

"I've already told everyone, but we're all taking a week off." He sighed. "Ted is still grieving Nathan, and I don't know how to help him."

"You're his best friend. That will help him. You just need to reach out and be there for him."

He gave me a side glance. "Thanks," he murmured, but the smile he gave wasn't genuine. The pain he harbored was seeping through.

"No problem. I know you were starved for blood, but

you seemed to be really out of it. You were mumbling a lot, like you were having a conversation. What was happening?"

"When I was hanging up there, I seemed to drift off. I honestly don't know what it was. One second, I was in the dark, smelly crypt, and then the next, a man in golden robes was standing before me."

"Do you think you were hallucinating?" I asked.

"Maybe, but it seemed too real. And it wasn't the first time. I've been having these vivid dreams since you fried me with your lightning on the way back from the mansion."

I placed my hand on his. "I'm so sorry. You should have told me."

He moved his hand out from under mine. "I was hoping eventually I could figure out how the dreams were connected."

I retracted my hand. "Why do you think they're connected? What are you searching for?"

His knuckles turned white around the bottle. "The truth." He downed another shot and poured another, holding the bottle out to me.

I whisked mine down and held the empty glass out. "That's not an answer."

"Heh, yeah, I know. They feel so real in the moment. I spoke to the God of Darkness." He chuckled nervously. "I kind of believed him when he told me he created the Chaos Brothers."

I downed another drink, holding my glass out as Luke refilled them both. It was a good liquor that didn't have the same effect on me like regular humans. Luke seemed to be the same way. Only Bob's drinks had been able to act faster than my fire could burn through it.

"He said I would remember everything in time."

"Whoa, like reincarnation?" I asked between sips of whiskey.

"Yeah, but he never came out and said it."

"Did you look into the Chaos Brothers more?"

Luke slammed his drink. "It seems throughout history when one dies, he resurfaces twenty-one years later. I don't know in what way, but it seems like I'm connected somehow."

"So, what're you going to do?" I asked, my stomach tightening as I waited for him to answer.

He whispered, "I don't know yet."

"Don't worry. According to my heritage, The Zodian Warrior can defeat the Chaos Brothers." I grinned. "Maybe we can discover the truth together."

He picked up the bottle, giving it a shake. Liquid swirled, and he poured us one last drink.

He pulled himself up from the chair. "One for the road." Towering above me, he handed me the glass.

We took slow, even steps, trying not to spill as we walked down the hall. He tipped forward when he stopped.

I grasped his chest to steady him and turned to meet his eyes. "What is it?"

"When you . . ." he started, and the glass tumbled from his hand. "When I drank from you, I saw something before I regained consciousness."

"Like a God of Darkness?" I smirked, stepping closer to him.

He picked up a strand of my hair, curling it around his finger. "No, you were dying. I was standing in a big room with stained-glass windows, the setting sun reflecting throughout." He held my eyes. "There were bodies lying around, and we were at the center of it all."

"I don't understand." *I'm dying? Did he see the future?*

"I stood in the middle of the room, surrounded by dead bodies. One of them was Rabon. But a woman knelt before me. We conversed, but I didn't understand what was being said until the end when I spoke out loud. 'My loyalty is yours.'"

I rose up on my toes. "Your loyalty?"

"I was compelled to say those words. It was so weird. But I don't know what the promise was. I think the woman was a Zodian. When her eyes landed on me, for a split second, I thought she was you. You could have been her sister. But then she burst into flames. After the fire disappeared, a baby lay in her place."

I giggled. "A baby? That's not possible." My eyes held onto his. "It couldn't have been me."

"The woman had a mark on her skin like yours."

"It's the symbol of my mother's tribe."

"Then why do you hide it?" He grabbed my wrist, but all he found was my bracelet, so he let it fall, and my glass rolled across the floor.

"My father was always paranoid and made sure I always had it covered?"

"I guess that's a valid reason now that we know about Rabon."

"Yeah, but he should have just told me everything in the first place."

"I just thought it was your favorite since you never took it off."

"It belonged to my mother."

He grinned, pulling me close to him. He leaned down to whisper, "What does the mark have to do with any of this?"

I stood there in his embrace, my eyes half closing. I leaned back to peer up at him. " I have no idea. I do know you've always been there for me, and I can trust you to be here for me." *What is wrong with me?* "I'm really, really sorry about leaving you at the altar. I was planning on calling you to tell you everything when I left, but I couldn't find my phone."

"Your dad had it." He released me.

I wobbled back, pointing. "That makes sense. He told me I had left it at home. I'm sorry for how I left things. I've come to realize that my father's not always right."

"Make sure you remember that for the future. Do what's best for you, not him, Ember."

"I will. I have to since I'm the Zodian Warrior."

Twenty-eight

LUKE

The warmth seeped down my body. *I've killed the Zodian Warrior. Ember.* I inhaled her cinnamon scent. A steady rhythm beat against my chest. *She's alive.* I squeezed her tight, feeling her warm breath against my neck. *She's safe.* I closed my eyes, but brutal images overtook me.

I contemplated the stormy sky and then my opponent —Ember. It shouldn't be this way. "I'm not him," I tried again, taking a step forward, but she rushed me.

Her fist aflame, I dodged one after the other, keeping one step ahead of her.

"Ember." I pleaded, "I'm not Istros."

She didn't relent, her fire turning bright blue. She raised her hand, lightning crackling before she fired. I jumped to the left, but I couldn't outrun the surge. The impact knocked me onto my front and I rolled onto my back. She stood over me, her hand poised to end me.

"Em, please."

Her hand stabbed down, and mine stabbed up. The crackling of her blue flame fizzled out, her eyes wide with shock. Ember fell into my arms. I swiped the hair out of her eyes, but she was already gone.

I pulled out my dagger that had pierced her heart. It didn't have to be this way.

I tried to shake the nightmare by opening my eyes.

From the corner of my eye, a dark figure appeared in the room. Before I could move, the small basement window above me shattered. Holding the blanket above us, I shielded Ember from the shards that rained down.

She awoke, her eyes wide and body tense below mine.

The overwhelming scent of burnt forest invaded my space. The comforter was ripped off us. My skin started tingling from the rays of sun shining through the busted window. I backed into the darkness of the bathroom doorway.

Christo leered over my bed and grabbed Ember's forearms, jerking her from it into the sunlight.

I hissed. *Why the fuck didn't I put a shutter on that window.*

"Christo?" Ember said, startled. "What are you doing here?"

She searched the room, and her eyes grew wider. She pulled against his hold.

"I should have known. He's been in your thoughts too much." His voice boomed in the room.

"What?"

"Did you have sex with him?" Chris spat, pointing in my direction.

Ember turned to see me. "Luke?" She shook her head. "No."

"Then why did I find you asleep in his arms?"

"How could you?" asked a woman.

Kaity.

My gaze darted to where she stood in the open doorway. Her hand covered her mouth as she moved her head back and forth between me and Ember and the bed. She turned and sprinted back the way she came.

"Kaity!" Ember yelled. "It's not what you think."

Ember tried to run after Kaity, but Christo gripped her arm tightly. I could see her skin already starting to bruise. I would talk to Kaity later. Right now Chris was the threat.

I jumped through the beams of sunlight, but before I landed, the two of them vanished from the room.

"Ember!" I yelled.

I raced through the halls, up the staircase, and burst into her room. The shutters were all down, and the room was veiled in darkness.

"Ember?"

She wasn't here. I slipped out my phone and tried calling her. A beeping chime came from downstairs.

I sprinted in the direction of the sound and found myself back in the doorway of my room. Her phone lay in a pool of sunshine on my coffee table. *Fuck the sun.*

Twenty-nine

EMBER

When our bodies materialized in Christo's room, I shrugged him off, now wide awake.

"What the hell did you think you were doing?" I yelled, pacing away from him.

I half turned and he pushed me into the wall.

"Agh."

His lips found mine, and he pulled at my shirt.

"Chris, stop." I tried to push him away.

"You are *mine*," he growled, his teeth scraping my neck as he snaked his hand into my hair.

With my palms flat against his hot, hard chest, I blasted him with a burst of heat. He skidded away from me, patting down what remained of his shirt.

"I said stop."

We stared at each other, breathing hard.

"You're so damn powerful," he breathed. "I was retrieving my *wife* from the arms of another man."

I clenched my fist, staring at the solid abs in front of

175

me. For what seemed like an eternity, my mind warred with my body. *Why can't I stay off you?*

I jumped into his arms. He hooked his arms under my butt to support my weight, and I wrapped my arms around his neck, snaking my fingers into his hair and pulling his mouth to mine. We devoured one another in the middle of the room, each enjoying the taste of the other.

Chris carried me to the bed, our lips never breaking contact. He laid me down, pressing his body into mine. His hands roamed every curve and crevice with an urgency. The heat between us rose, breaths quickening as our kisses deepened.

I tugged at his belt, desperate to feel him closer, to have nothing between us. He helped, swiftly discarding his pants and then mine. Our clothes fell to the floor in scattered heaps. His hands explored me, and I reveled in the sensation, arching into his touch.

"You're so beautiful," he murmured against my skin, his voice rough with desire.

His words sent shivers down my spine, making me ache for him even more.

I pulled him closer with a fervent need, our bodies finally meeting. We moved together, a perfect rhythm, our bond connecting us more, deepening with every touch—every kiss. The world outside ceased to exist; it was only us, wrapped in this moment of raw passion.

His name escaped my lips in a breathless whisper as we reached our peak together, bodies trembling with the intensity. He held me close, our hearts pounding in unison, as we slowly came down from the high.

For a moment, we lay there, tangled in each other's arms, the silence filled only with our heavy breathing. I traced circles on his chest, feeling a sense of peace I hadn't felt often.

With half my body draped over Christo, my head lying in the crook of his arm, I closed my eyes and slowly traced "Do I love you?" as he dozed.

"I love you too," he muttered.

My eyes snapped open. "What?"

He shifted under me, rolling onto his side so that our faces were inches apart. "You traced 'I love you' on my chest."

My cheeks warmed at his words. "I hope you know I didn't do anything with Luke. We just got too drunk." I propped myself up on my elbow. "We only passed out in the same bed. There's truly nothing between us. It was puppy love, but we're still good friends."

His eyes opened. "I know." He closed them again.

I poked him in the chest. "You were mad two hours ago, and now you know."

He rolled onto his back, pulling me on top of him. My legs settled around him as he hardened beneath my core.

"When you pushed me away earlier," he started, sliding his length into me, "our connection deepened, and well, I just knew."

He smiled, moving beneath me.

"Ah." I ground my body into his, leaning down to kiss

his lips softly, taking my time while his hands explored my butt and thighs.

                         —

Several hours later, I threw on Christo's shirt and walked out of the bedroom, eager to find something to alleviate the rumble in my stomach. I only had to turn around twice in my search for the kitchen. It wasn't like I had spent a lot of time outside of his room.

The large kitchen windows filtered in the natural light. I stopped short. A woman stood behind the center island, drinking a cup of coffee. She glared at me.

I pulled down Christo's shirt. "Hello."

"Are you the newest plaything?" she asked before turning back to the paper that lay on the counter.

Plaything. "I'm Ember."

"Mom," Christo said from somewhere behind me.

Mom. This was his mom.

She came around the island and waited as Christo kissed her on each cheek before she went back to her coffee.

"I didn't know you would be here," he said, moving closer to me. He reached around my waist, pulling me to his side. "I could have come to see you at your house if you would have just messaged."

The hem of the shirt rose, and I grasped the bottom, trying to stretch it over my naked ass. I wiggled in Christo's arms, but he tightened his hold so I couldn't escape.

His mom flicked the paper. "I have matters to discuss with you that couldn't wait for you to decide to visit your mother."

"What is it?"

She eyed me. "You can go now."

I gasped "Huh" at her tone. I didn't want to be here anyway, but she could have been nicer. I gazed up at Christo.

Turning on my heels, I said, "I'll head back now."

He leaned down and kissed the top of my head.

"Mom," Christo said.

"She's a human. Could you disgrace this family anymore?"

I turned back, watching the shadows on the wall. *Human?*

Thirty

EMBER

The next day, I stood on Kaity's front porch since she wouldn't take my calls. *Who is taking my calls these days?*

She opened the door and immediately tried to shut it, but I stuck my foot in the way.

"I don't want to talk to you, Ember," she said, backing into the room.

I followed her. "I know, but I came to tell you what really happened."

She stomped down the hallway. "I saw what happened."

"You did?" I said, chasing her into the kitchen. "Are you sure? Because I'm pretty sure both of us still had all our clothes on."

She stopped to look at me.

"See? Maybe you don't know what happened." I sighed, scrubbing my face. "You have to believe me. I'll do whatever you want. Truth spell, serum, whatever magic you want to use. I really can't lose you as a friend. I promise you nothing happened."

She tsked. "You'll let me mix a serum?"

"Yes." I waited.

Kaity stood silent for a few seconds and then gave me a short nod.

"How long will it take to make one?"

"I already have some made."

"Oh, that's handy."

She filled up her tea kettle with water. Once filled, she placed it on the stove to heat. She opened a locked cabinet and pulled out a small vial. She set the bottle down on the counter between us, and I stepped back. The silvery gray liquid swirled.

The vial was so similar to the one Dad had given me for my birthday. I leaned in, eyeing the tint of the liquid. Dad's had been murky and dark, giving it an ominous presence whenever I'd been near it. Kaity's shimmered like the moon reflecting off a lake.

I trust Kaity.

Once the tea was brewed, she tipped the vial's content into the cup she sat in front of me. "It'll be a bit bitter."

I picked up the mug and brought it to my lips. I paused before setting it back down.

"I knew you wouldn't do it," she said, shaking her head.

"No, I just want to tell you something before I drink this." She looked at me, and I took a deep breath. "Luke and I . . . We used to date. It was much more than that though. He had asked me to marry him once when we were young. Barely eighteen."

"What? How did I not know that?"

"I think it broke his heart a little. Ted and Grace weren't happy with me when I skipped town. But I knew that one day I might put him in danger, so I chose to leave on the day we were supposed to marry."

I picked up the tea, now slightly chilled, and tipped the contents back, biting down on the bitterness until it was all gone.

"Ask me anything," I said, setting the cup down into the sink.

She thought for a minute. "Did you have sex with Luke?"

"Yes," I said.

"Lair, you said you didn't."

"Wait, I have had sex with him, but we didn't do anything last night."

"Okay. So you didn't have sex with Luke *last night?* Why did we find you in his bed this morning?"

"We got to talking in the cafeteria and started drinking this whiskey he'd received. We downed the whole bottle, and as we were walking to our rooms, we stopped again to chat. I don't remember much after that. It all got fuzzy, but I know we didn't have sex. We were still both fully dressed in the clothes we had on yesterday."

"Uh-huh." She crossed her arms. "Do you love Luke?"

"I do love him, but I'm not in love with him."

"You love Chris?"

"No," I uttered. "I mean, yes." I sighed. "It's complicated."

She laid her hand on top of mine. "Whose isn't." She gave me a great, big grin. "What were you talking about that got you both so drunk?"

I shrugged. "About Rabon capturing Luke and how he's trying to make Luke believe he's Istros. We talked about my mark," I said, pointing to my exposed wrist.

I gasped. I'd left my bracelet at Christo's when I'd showered earlier this morning.

Silence greeted me. I turned to Kaity. Her eyes were wide.

"What did you say?"

"My mark, it's right here." I pointed at it.

"No, that Luke is Istros."

"No, Rabon called him Istros at the mansion and when he kidnapped Luke. He wants Luke to join him as part of the Chaos Brothers."

"Did he tell you all this?"

I shook my head. "No, I found out when Rabon called him Istros in that crypt." I smiled. "I don't know if he would have told me otherwise."

"How could he deal with that by himself?" Kaity asked, grabbing my arm, and the room skewed.

Once my feet were on solid ground again, I had to brace myself on my knees, my head spinning and stomach turning.

Nope. Kaity had brought us to the cafeteria.

I raced into the kitchen and found a trash can before the contents of my stomach came back up.

My hair was lifted out of my face, and Kaity stood behind me. "Sorry, I forget that serum sometimes acts differently depending on the magic that happens around it." She handed me a towel off the counter.

I wiped my mouth and went to the sink. After turning on the faucet, I cupped my hands to drink. I felt better after washing out my mouth.

"Okay?"

"Yeah. Does that mean the serum is out of my system?"

Kaity pursed her lips. "Depends, but most likely. And since your magic is centered around fire, I'm sure your body will burn it off faster."

"What are you two doing here?" Luke asked from the doorway. "I gave everyone the week off, and no one took it. Ted was here earlier trying to track down any remaining vampire nests. I had to confiscate his stakes to get him to go home."

Kaity stalked up to him. "How could you not tell me about what's happening with you and Rabon?"

Luke grimaced at me. "I thought we were keeping that between us for now."

I crossed my arms. "And what happened to being honest with everyone?"

"Fine." He sighed, turning back to Kaity. "I don't know what the truth is." He motioned for us to sit down, and he told Kaity what we talked about.

"Okay, can it be true?" Kaity asked.

"I hope not," said Luke.

Thirty-one

KAITY

"You've been having visions? Does that mean your memories are coming back?" I asked, tapping my fingers on the table.

Luke shook his head. "I've been having dreams and hallucinations. I don't think they're memories, really. I can't be Istros."

I stole a look over at Ember. *Could he be Istros?* Her body was tense, and I could tell she didn't quite believe him. She'd noted that he'd been acting weird these last few months. Nathan's death had affected us all in different ways, but I knew Luke could find a way through his grief.

"We should find a way to kill Rabon," Ember said. "It would give us twenty-one years to find a more permanent death."

We sat in silence after Ember's suggestion.

"I think that would be our last resort if we can't find another solution to end him for good sooner," Luke said.

"But if you *are* Istros, then we have to find a way to do it without killing you too," I added.

Luke tensed at my suggestion, and Ember glanced away. *What are they hiding?*

I started tapping my fingers again and stopped. "Oh, I got it!" They turned in my direction. "There's a spell in my grimoire that deals with memories. Just a sec."

I snapped into my bedroom with a small jolt of magic and grabbed my spell book from the bedside table. With another snap of magic, I popped back to the school in record time.

Flipping through the pages, I skimmed the text until I found the spell that dealt with memories. "This will let me go into a memory with you."

"We could all see what happened the day Rabon became a Chaos Brother?" Luke asked.

I shook my head. *Not how magic works.* "No. We can only see memories of the people connected to the spell."

"What about that vision you had?" Ember asked. "The one you were telling me about?"

I jumped in my seat. "That would be perfect! If you already know some of the details, we can drill into it."

"All right," Luke said, leaning on his elbows on the table. "How do we do this?"

I read more from the grimoire that was stuffed full like an old scrapbook. "Here it is." I ran my finger down the page. "I have all the ingredients at home. Meet me in the gym."

I left them sitting at the table to gather the supplies from home and teleported back to the gym with a farmers' market bag full of the reagents I would need. I started to raise my hand in greeting but paused at the concern on Luke's face.

"Are you okay?" Luke asked, moving closer to Ember.

He grabbed her arm, brushing the T-shirt sleeve up. A hand-print-sized bruise encircled her arm like a purple band.

"He hurt you," he whispered.

Ember shrugged, making his hand drop away. "I'm fine. I took care of it." She winked.

Well, at least she handled it.

Luke rubbed the bridge of his nose. "He's not good for you, Ember."

Ember crossed her arms. "Why do you guys keep telling me what's good or not good for me? I can make my *own* choices."

"Only she knows who is good for her," I said, gaining their attention.

"Never mind," Luke huffed, exasperated.

All right then.

I sat down with the supplies and put a bowl in the center.

"I'll chant the words. Luke, you'll need to focus on the memory you saw. Sit with me in a comfortable position so we can hold hands. Our connection to Luke's memory will be linked through our contact. Em, could you light the candle?" I asked.

She smiled, snapping her fingers, and the wick was set aflame.

I placed the rest of the ingredients in the bowl around the flickering candle.

I set my hands on my knees, and they intertwined their fingers with mine. I started to chant the Latin phrases, repeating the spell three times over.

Momenta pereunt in tempore.
Veritatem animarum nostrarum revela.
Et nos adiuva in codicellos imple.

At first, nothing seemed to happen, but soon, my eyes grew heavy, and it was becoming harder and harder to stay upright. Luke and Ember were giant blurs.

I blinked, sitting straighter and glancing around my surroundings. I was on a lake bed, and sand gritted against my skin. My jeans and shirt had been replaced with a flimsy dress. I covered my breasts and stood.

"Tesia."

I turned at the sound, but my vision blurred. My stomach dropped, and I hunched forward. When I stood up, fluorescent lights shone down on me. The smell of the boy's locker room assaulted my nose.

"Kaity," they said, clearer this time.

I speculated, trying to locate its source, but the room seemed empty. Panic surged through me. I had no idea how I got here.

"Who's there?" I called out, my voice trembling.

The lights flickered around me before a figure emerged. It was Luke. He was exactly the same but different.

As he approached, I could hear childlike voices, and I knew where I was.

Four years ago, I had wanted to learn self-defense, but the only comparable class was boxing. It wasn't until I showed up for the first class that I knew I'd read the flyer incorrectly. I'd signed up for a children's class.

The class faded, and again, my stomach did a somersault. I knew exactly where I was this time. The back alley behind the local Y where Luke taught boxing. The last time I saw him alive.

"Let's talk after my weekend, okay?" he said.

I rushed forward. "No, don't go."

He didn't seem fazed by my plea.

"Kaity, I'm sorry. But I really need to go now. We leave early in the morning."

"That's what I'm talking about," I yelled. "Your parents will die if you take that trip."

"Really, Kaity, just give me time to think."

I stood dumbfounded. He was saying the same exact words as the first time, but I wasn't. *Why isn't he hearing me?*

"Luke!" I tried again, but he faded away, and then the alley dissipated.

I could feel Luke's and Ember's hands holding mine and hear their solid breathing. I opened my eyes. They were still in the memories. Ember's forehead was wrinkled while Luke's shoulders were hunched over. *What are they seeing?*

Thirty-two

LUKE

I stood on a balcony facing the fading sun. Its dimming rays didn't bother me, but there was enough light to still see. I didn't know why I was here. But Kaity's spell had to have worked. Memories resurfaced at a fast rate. Below me sat the city of Anu, the Zodian capital. I hadn't wanted to come, but Rabon insisted we get to the bottom of the whispers that had spread over the last seventeen years. *A Zodian born of this bloodline will end the Chaos.*

Nothing I'd found had ended this curse of my existence. I'd already lived 300 years without Tesia.

Something moved to my left, and I half turned to a young woman dressed in a flowing purple gown.

"Would you like to come in?" she asked, gesturing with her hand.

I followed her into the large bedroom, decorated in plain white. "You know who I am?"

"Istros," she said, turning to face me. "But I do not know what it is you want."

"The rumor . . ."

She cut me off. "It is true."

"It's you that we seek." Rabon had been searching for this girl, obsessed with finding her before she could kill us.

She nodded. "What is it you want?" she asked again.

I let loose a breath. "Freedom," I muttered to myself. *Death.*

She stepped closer, pulling out something hidden in the layers of her gown. "I will help you, but in return, you will pledge your fealty." A ring sat in the center of the palm she held out to me. "This is a token of my goodwill. It shall help you in the daylight as long as my blood is alive."

I reached to take the ring. It was cast from iron, a collection of jewels set into the top. A center diamond was surrounded by a ruby, emerald, citrine, and sapphire, each gem representing the ways of the Zodian people. I tested the weight of the ring before sliding it onto my index finger.

A young man around her age skidded into the room.

"Serafina! Rabon is attacking. We must get you to safety." His mouth hung open when he saw me.

She smiled at me before turning to the man. "I know, Cara Anu. We only have a few minutes." She turned back to me, motioning with her hands. "Come with me."

Princess Serafina and the young man walked out of the room holding hands. Screams erupted from the people fleeing my brother. I fought against the crowd, losing Serafina. Instead, I followed the cries to find my brother. Standing on the interior balcony overlooking the madness, I spotted the Zodian king and queen facing off against Rabon. The princess was nowhere in sight. *Has she gotten away? Can I trust her to help me? Is she truly the key that my brother thinks she is?*

Not long into the fight, the king fell, and the queen soon after.

"You will never have her," she yelled as Rabon plunged his sword into her chest.

He laughed. "I'll find her even if it takes a million years, but I don't have to." He turned.

I followed Rabon's gaze to see the princess standing on the edge of the ballroom. Blood soaked the hem of her dress nearly to her knees. She stood so still, looking at her fallen parents.

"I see you found me," Rabon hissed, taking small, measured steps toward her.

She widened her stance. "I will be your end."

Rabon roared, running at her. She sidestepped, bringing forth a sword with her magic.

I watched from above. *She is well trained.*

She twisted out of my brother's radius, snaking her lithe body and dodging the broad sword Rabon wielded. *But is she the savior I need?*

Rabon pinned his blade into her shoulder, and the princess screamed. Rabon laughed, but he hadn't heard what I had—her determination. Serafina let out a war cry and engulfed her entire body in flames.

Rabon tried to flee the fire, but she wrapped her

hands around the sword he was holding and pulled him closer.

He began to burn.

Once her fires died out, Serafina stood while Rabon's charred corpse slumped to the ground. She reached for the hilt of the sword stuck in her body and grunted as she pulled. With a step forward, she leaned her hand on Rabon's shoulder and aimed the tip of the sword at his heart. She paused long enough to glance up at me before plunging it into his chest.

Rabon's essence faded from the room.

I jumped over the balcony and landed beside my brother's remains. I pulled up his corpse, staring into his dead eyes before flinging his body across the room.

I turned to the princess. "My loyalty is yours."

Blood seeped from the wound in her shoulder, her knees gave out, and she sank to the ground. "You will be bonded to my bloodline. As long as you protect and keep my blood alive, we will help you gain the freedom you seek."

"I am your enemy, after all," I said. "You are putting a lot of faith in me,"

She loosed a raspy laugh. "I don't have anything else left to lose."

"We all have *something* left to lose."

"For me, that is you." Her words were like an edict. "The prophecy *will* become real. I've met her. She just needs time. And your protection will give her that."

We stood as the last bit of light faded from the room.

"Istros, my blood is your only salvation for the future," she said finally.

That very blood pooled at her feet.

"I will protect the bloodline—until the prophecy is fulfilled."

Serafina cut her palm with a knife and held it out to me. I reciprocated. She pressed her wound to mine, and then flames engulfed her once more. Though they did not burn my skin as they swirled around her.

Her eyes brightened, looking out through the flames. "Deliver her to the Irra Shaman."

Deliver who?

The flames died down. The princess was no more. A small cry sounded from the floor. A tiny pink baby lay in the pool of blood. Serafina was gone from this world, but her bloodline remained.

Thirty-three

EMBER

The gym exhaust fan faded into the background, and I forced my eyelids to open. A glittering ballroom greeted me. Couples were dancing with rainbow colors raining down on them through the stained-glass windows that went from ceiling to floor. A group of four musicians stood in the corner playing a quiet melody as voices and laughter drifted over the room.

I stood alone on the side of the dance floor. *Where are Luke and Kaity? I need to find them. Did I jump into Luke's memory—no, Istros's memory—by myself?*

A woman passed me, and my body shimmered. I watched my hand, seeing through it for a second before it solidified again. I turned to the man next to me, touching him on the shoulder. While I could feel his body, he seemed to not notice I was there. I waved in front of his face, but there was no response. The people couldn't see me. I searched for Luke or Kaity again. As my eyes traveled over the ballroom, a tightness settled in the pit of my stomach. The aether warned me. Rabon stood in the shadows.

I grabbed the man's wrist, but my hand passed through him. I caught sight of a mark. My mark. He was part of my tribe. I scanned the rest of the room. All or most of them had the same mark. They were all my people. I tried again to get their attention, waving my arms back and forth.

"Rabon is here. You all need to leave," I yelled, but no one listened.

Luke's familiar presence flowed around me. He was here. I tried to determine where it was coming from and then sprinted into the hallway. There were fewer people here in the halls and back through the kitchens. I followed the smell of sweat, a familiar one I remembered from high school, back through more halls.

"Oh dear," a voice said in front of me after I rounded a corner.

I came to a stop. She looked like me. *Was this the lady Luke had seen in his vision?*

"You're not supposed to be here," she said, grabbing my arm and pulling me into the closest room.

"You can see me." *Touch me.*

She gave me a weird look and released me.

"Well, no one else can see me."

She smiled. "They haven't developed the aether as well as we have."

"Who are you?" I asked.

"Serafina," she said. "This confirms I'm right. He will do the right thing."

"What?" *Who?*

"Never mind, dear." She grasped my shoulders, bringing me into a hug. "I love you," she whispered.

"I love you too?" I said, warmth spreading to my heart.

"I'm sorry. It's going to be hard."

"What?" I asked. "What do you mean?"

She shook her head. "It was so nice to meet you, Ember."

The door opened. "Princess."

I stood looking at the newcomer. He didn't seem to see me, but I saw him. I wanted to say his name, but I knew it wasn't him. That didn't make sense, but the similarity in their faces was astonishing.

"Why are you here? The king said we need to go now."

Serafina smiled. "I know what he said, but I can't leave just yet. I haven't made my pact with him."

"This is ridiculous."

"I'll be ready in a moment," she said.

He nodded and closed the door.

"Who was that?" I asked.

"One of my protectors. They want me to run," she huffed.

"You're tired of running." I finished for her.

She nodded. "It's been all I've ever done, and I'm

ready to settle down." She put her hand on her stomach, and I noticed she had a small bump. "But I know everything will work out."

"How?" I asked.

Screams pierced through the walls of the room.

"It's already started."

I'm too late. I can't warn anyone.

"It wasn't your place. This is but a memory," she stated, walking to the door.

Before I could respond, she darted out of the room. I chased after her, retracing my steps down the hallway, through the kitchen, and back to the ballroom. The room was no longer glittering but drenched in blood.

Rabon stood in the middle of the room, Zodians dead at his feet. He smirked as he stared down Serafina. She stood tall on the other side of the room.

I stepped into the room, but Serafina's eyes held me still. She shook her head ever so slightly and then tilted it up. I turned to the balcony where she stared. *Luke.* The force holding me in place dissipated, and I headed for the second floor. I went back into the hallway, taking a different path and finding the stairs. Climbing them two at a time, I reached the balcony before the fight began. Stepping out, I realized it wasn't Luke but Istros.

He didn't notice me as I stepped out onto the balcony. He was fixated on the fight below. I leaned against the railing, watching as Serafina kicked Rabon's ass. She was magnificent and used all four elements to her advantage. The ground turned into quicksand as she threw giant balls of fire at him. He would get out of one trick and land in the next. But he was fast, and, in a rage, he plunged a sword into her shoulder.

"No," I gasped.

Serafina locked eyes with me, a smile on her lips as she pulled Rabon closer to her body and lit them both on fire. Tears rained down my cheeks. *She did it.* As the fire died, Rabon fell to the ground. His eyes glossed over. Serafina grasped the sword handle and pulled it out of her shoulder.

Istros jumped down from the balcony and picked up Rabon before tossing his body like a doll. He stood in front of Serafina. She gave me a weak smile before she sank to her knees. *No!* I rushed back down the stairs, through the hallway, and into the ballroom, jumping over the dead bodies to reach her side, but her body was engulfed in flames once more.

"Serafina!" I cried.

A pull came over me, and the stillness of the ballroom faded into the hum of the gym exhaust fan once more. I sat in the circle with Luke and Kaity. We all sat in silence, looks of contemplation on each of our faces.

I unclasped my hands from theirs. "Where were you two?" No one answered. "I saw the fall of Anu."

Kaity seemed to jump back to the present. "What Sofia and Jasmine had talked about?"

"Yeah, it had to be. Rabon and Istros killed all of my people that day."

Luke tensed.

"Sorry," I said.

He shook his head. "No, you're right. I was there but

like a passenger in Istros's body. I couldn't control what he did. Just followed along as everything happened."

"Did you see me? I stood on the balcony with him," I said, standing and stretching my stiff body.

Luke stood too. "No." He shook his head and started out of the gym.

"Where are you going?" I asked.

"I need to think."

"You need to tell us what you saw. It seems we all saw different things. Kaity?" I turned to her.

She was still sitting on the floor. Her cheeks turned pink.

"The spell didn't really work for me," she said.

I turned back to Luke to see his eyebrow rise, but he shrugged and left the room.

"Luke!" I yelled, running after him. I caught up with him on the stairs. The cafeteria door stood open at the bottom. I could hear voices inside. "Luke, we need to talk about this."

He wouldn't look me in the eyes. "There's nothing to talk about. Istros slaughtered all of your people."

I grabbed his arm. "It's fine. We need to understand what took place so we can put a stop to Rabon."

He pulled his arm from my grasp and started down the stairs again.

"Luke, I saw you. I saw Istros talk to Serafina."

He turned to look at me and huffed. "Istros promised to protect her blood."

"Protect her blood," Kaity said from behind me. "Her entire bloodline? That would include Ember."

Luke locked eyes with me before nodding. This closeness we always had was the result of Istros's promise. "In exchange, her bloodline will help me break the curse."

How? I had no idea. "You mean me?" I said.

He nodded before disappearing.

"Luke," I yelled, but he didn't come back. I turned back to Kaity. "How do we break a curse we know nothing about?"

She shrugged. "I don't know. I'm exhausted though. I'm going home, and I'll think about it in my nice warm bed."

Light shimmered around her before she disappeared too.

"Bye," I muttered, heading into the cafeteria.

Kaity seemed to be hiding something. I wanted to question what she saw.

Luke didn't take the memory spell the way I expected either. He wanted the truth, and now he had it. He seemed more indifferent.

Bob and his friends sat at the bar. They were quiet when I entered, so they obviously heard everything we'd discussed.

"It is true, then," Chase said.

"What is?" I asked, sitting next to him.

"That Luke really is Istros?" Scout asked.

"Appears that way," I said, grabbing the drink Bob put in front of me. I glanced at the handmade garland wrapped around the bar. *Are they going to celebrate*

Christmas? I downed the contents and wrinkled my forehead. "This is water."

"It's ten in the morning, Ember," Bob said, filling the glass again.

"But," I started.

Bob gave me a stern look.

"Fine." I drank the water before leaving.

Thirty-four

EMBER

A few hours later, I trudged over the mossy ground leading up to Dad's front porch.

I knocked on the door, and footsteps sounded inside the house. The door swung open, and Dad pressed against the screen door. His eyes widened when they landed on me.

"Emma," he said. "What happened? You and Chris didn't show."

"Hey," I said.

Is he going to let me in? Considering he had yet to open the screen door between us, I doubted he would. My fists tightened at my sides. The progress I'd seemed to make with him was likely back to zero.

"Sorry, something came up."

"What, Ember?" he asked, my given name coming out harsh. "Something to do with the supernatural?" His eyes landed on my right shoulder. "You're bleeding."

My eyes fell to where my jacket had fallen open.

"I told you that life will only put you in danger."

Whether there was concern in his voice or not, I couldn't tell. But his eyes blazed with hatred. He tilted back a drink I hadn't noticed in his hand. Amber liquid swirled around the glass. I had never seen him drunk before.

Truth. I needed to tell him the truth.

"Luke was kidnapped by Rabon," I started, and before he could cut me off, I rambled on. "I got caught by his demons, and they threw me in a crypt with him. He was forced to drink my blood. Obviously he didn't kill me. That's why I couldn't meet you that morning. I was recovering, and Chris was watching over me."

"Chris?" he asked, rubbing his face. "He knows you're supernatural." He blew out a long breath. "I should've known."

"Yes. He's a demon," I said, omitting the Immortal part. What difference would it make to my dad?

"Ember, don't you see they will bring you to your death?"

I unclenched my fingers. "What will bring me to my death are lies. If you had told me more about my past—more about my mother when I asked—would any of this have happened?" I asked, and he stepped back as I pushed forward. "You've kept me from everything that makes me who I am. Why can't you just love *me*?" The air around me heated with each word.

His eyes soften at my question. "I just wanted you to be happy. To be normal. To live a normal life, unlike her.

You can't expect any man to love you when you're like this."

Silence fell between us.

"I do love you, Em," he said. "I always will, but you need to ask yourself if this is all worth it."

Before I could say anything else, he backed into the room and started to close the door. I yanked the screen open and pushed hard against the wooden door. Dad staggered back at the resistance, and liquid from the glass he'd been holding sloshed onto the floor, drenching his hand. The smell of alcohol lingered on his breath. He switched the glass to his other hand and then proceeded to wipe his wet fingers on his shirt.

"Dad, why are you drinking in the middle of the day?" I asked, coming into the house.

It was a disaster compared to what was normal for him. Papers were scattered on several surfaces, and For Sale signs leaned against the counter and the fridge.

Dad headed toward the living room, and I followed him. He sank into his favorite chair, tossing back the remains of his drink. Clumsily, he traded his glass for a photo from the side table that wasn't normally there.

"It's not the middle of the day," he muttered, eyes locked on the picture.

I eyed the near-empty bottle of whiskey that sat on the floor by his chair. "It looks like you've been drinking for more than a day. You never drink. What gives?" I stepped closer, catching a glimpse of the frame.

It was the one from his bedroom with his family standing outside a church. From what I'd gathered over the years, it was the last picture they had taken as a family before his sister died.

He picked up the nearly empty bottle, but I grabbed it before he started to pour.

"Dad," I started, crouching down to his level. "What's wrong?"

His eyes remained on the photo. "She was too young," he said. "They both were."

"Your sister?"

Dad nodded, and tears began streaking down his face —a stark contrast to the man who'd raised me. "We didn't know any better. We were just playing with our friends." He sniffled. "I didn't know what was happening until she just lay there—on the grass, not moving."

Is today the anniversary of her death? I had no idea. He never shared this with me growing up—never mourned her death when I was around.

"I'm so sorry about your sister."

He lifted his eyes to mine, but there wasn't the sadness I expected in them.

"Now you're one of *them*," he said, his voice coming out like venom. "Get out of my house!" he yelled, pushing himself up from the chair.

I scrambled back, tripping over my feet and landing on my rear. "Dad?"

He stood over me. "Get out of my house!"

Reeling from my confrontation with Dad, I headed to the only other place that had always provided comfort—Grace's. I parked by the old barn where we used to play hide-and-seek and have sleepovers. It was my refuge during my teenage years when life with Dad had become unbearable.

The lights were on in the house as I walked up the back stairs. Grace's mom stood in the kitchen with her apron on. Seeing me coming, she opened the door and gave me a big warm hug.

"I didn't know you were back in town."

"Oh," I said, confused since I'd been back for half a year now. "Yeah, um, is Grace home?"

Her mom nodded like I knew she would since Grace's car was parked outside.

"I'm just going to go on up."

"Oh, dear, take the last of the chocolate chip cookies with you." She held out a plate of her county-famous cookies. "I'm making more."

I accepted the plate and thanked her as I headed to Grace's room.

"Hey," I said, coming into the room to sit on her bed.

She sat at her vanity, red lipstick in hand, and turned to face me, her makeup half done. "I'm glad you're here!"

"Your mom's baking more cookies," I said, setting the plate on the bed.

"She's always baking something when they're home." She turned and started applying her lipstick. She opened her mouth wide, and her eyes mimicked the movement.

"I wanted to talk about Chris," she said, capping the lipstick.

"Sure. We can talk about him," I said. "Do you have time? I really need to vent about Dad too."

It was after seven, and she was clearly getting ready for something.

"Oh, I have a date," she said, continuing to put on makeup. "But I have time for you."

She rubbed perfume on her wrist and behind her ears.

My body relaxed, and I told her about my latest run-in with Dad while she worked on her hair. "I don't understand why he can't forgive me for choosing to be myself."

Closing my eyes, I breathed in and out slowly, listening to the clicks of Grace's curling iron.

"I'm sure he'll come around. Remember when you went through that phase where you wanted to wear dresses, and he had a total meltdown?" She grinned at my reflection in the mirror.

I smiled at the memory. I'd been about thirteen when I bought my first dress and loved it so much that I went to yard sales all summer, haggling over prices for newer dresses. Dad kept telling me I couldn't protect myself in a dress. After several weeks of him complaining, I went out one afternoon and proved him wrong. He still didn't like the idea of me wearing dresses all the time, so we compromised and agreed that I would only wear dresses to church on Sunday. *Why am I always the one giving in to what he wants?*

I wouldn't yield this time. I enjoyed my powers and was better at controlling them in fights while using martial arts. Protecting people and making the world a better place for everyone was my calling. I loved doing this. I liked myself better this way.

"Ember, he'll come around. He loves you," Grace said, looking back at me, her blonde curls bouncing.

"I'm really starting to wonder," I confessed, lying back on the bed, nudging the cookies beside me.

I'd never seen Dad so drunk before or openly discussing his family history.

"Now for Chris," she said in a matter-of-fact voice.

I sat back up and turned to face her. "What about him?"

Grabbing a black tube of mascara, she half turned away and slowly twisted it open, biting the inside of her bottom lip.

"He's a demon," she said finally.

I nodded, catching her eye in the mirror as she brushed the black liquid onto her lashes. "I know."

"You can't date him."

"You can't lump all demons into one evil circle. They're not all the same. Look at Bob, Scout, and Chase. They're super different and are basically harmless. I thought you'd see that by now."

She put down the mascara and stood, facing me. "Well, Chris is *not* harmless. You do remember what those girls said about him four months ago, right?"

Yes. I remembered. Jasmine had spread the story in the cafeteria that Christo had slaughtered a room full of demons in mere minutes. The image that popped into my head wasn't pretty, but I had yet to talk to Christo about that incident. I wasn't going to judge him until I could get his side of the story. It wasn't fair to him since all he'd done was be helpful these past months.

"Ember," Grace said, her voice harder than before.

My attention snapped to her. "Please don't be upset with me for who I'm dating. I've never told you who not to date, even though Steve was unpredictable."

Grace closed her eyes and took a deep breath. "I'm not mad. It's just that *you* have to be careful. You've done so much good in this world since getting your powers back. I don't want some piece of ass to get in the way. The world needs *you* even if they don't know it yet."

I cringed and stood. *What would she say if that piece of ass had been the problem in the first place?* If she knew how Chris and I actually got together, even though it was going well now, she would flip out.

"I understand, and he won't get in the way of me doing good for the world." I walked toward the door as Grace turned back to her vanity and sat down.

She probably needed to leave soon to make her date on time.

"Good. I'm so glad you're going to dump his ass."

I stopped. "I'm not ending the relationship." Especially since I couldn't—not that Grace needed to know that yet.

It was surprising I hadn't felt the need to tell her what had happened. I'd always told her everything before

I left for Berkeley. Maybe those four years had damaged our sisterlike relationship more than I realized.

My other growing concern was how close Grace had become with the Collective—her mentors. *Maybe that's why I don't want to share more with her.*

Over the last couple of weeks, I'd read about them in my mother's journal. The way she referenced the Collective made me question their true intent for the world. *Are they really here to help?* I didn't know yet, but it was something I would look into for Grace's sake. Mentioning anything now wouldn't help her believe me, so I was going to wait until I gathered more evidence.

Grace paused applying her eyeliner to face me, one eye done and the other bare. "You have to. It's what the Collective wants. *You* can't be tangled up with some demon."

"I'm not sure why who I am dating matters to the Collective. And I don't work for them. I don't have to do anything they say." She opened her mouth to speak, but I cut her off. "He may be a demon, but he's not a monster. He has feelings like everyone else. And I won't shut the door in his face because otherworldly beings think they know what's best for me. I've been trying to get away from that shit all my life," I said, each word getting louder, but this time, I managed to keep the heat in the room stable.

"You have to understand that the Collective knows the world is leaning on you." She stood and took a step toward me. "It means that if you have to forgo sex for the greater good, then start forgoing, sister."

I couldn't believe the person in front of me was my best friend. We'd gone through every broken relationship together until I'd walked out on Luke. That was the start of our crack.

"God, is this about when I left Luke?"

"About Luke?" She crossed her arms over her chest. "No, this is about you dating a demon and all your senses being manipulated. He's a *demon*, and he's charming you. Snap out of it, Em."

Charming me.

"I don't know what you want me to say. I'm not ending it with Chris." I turned and headed for the door.

There was no reason to continue this conversation. I peeked back at Grace on the way through the door. In the reflection of the vanity mirror, she jutted out her chin, and her hair covered her eyes. Without another word, I left.

I played the radio loud on the drive home, hoping to drown out my thoughts.

Is Parker Elementary my home now?

Thirty-five

EMBER

It seemed easier to dwell on how I was going to get to Berkeley on Friday than Grace and Dad. I'd managed to switch my afternoon shift for a morning one, but I still had to work on Friday, and there was no way I could make a thirteen-hour drive before the shop closed. Driving was out of the question.

I'd already asked Christo. Unfortunately, he was busy all day with Elder business. The only other option was for me to use Agni. I was afraid I would be too exhausted once I got there to get back. There was also the small, pesky problem of possibly catching something on fire. I'd already ruined two sweaters and a pair of pants in my attempts and kept a spare set of clothes in my car now. Most recently, I'd managed to go from the school to the range. *It's happening less and less now.*

I walked through the back entrance of the bank to clock in for my afternoon shift and headed to my station. It was only a half day, but it seemed to drag on from one elderly customer to the next. Occasionally, I'd have to keep my eyes down to avoid a grouchy one.

"Hi, Ember," someone I knew called out.

I grinned at Kaity's smiling face. "Hey, what can I help you with today?"

She slid a withdrawal slip over to me, and I began to process her request.

Looking at the computer screen, I asked, "What are you doing tonight?"

I knew she had the night off from patrol.

"Oh, well, I thought I would watch a movie. But . . ." She darted her head around. "I was wondering if you had time to practice tonight?"

I nodded, counting out the money and laying it in front of her. "Yeah, I can probably squeeze in an hour or two, except I'll need a bite to eat first."

I pulled an envelope out for the cash.

She waved it off. "What time do you clock out?"

I checked the time in the corner of the computer screen. "Another hour."

"Come to my place, and I'll cook dinner," she said, stuffing the money into her wallet. "Then we can practice."

"Sounds good. I'll bring dessert."

With that, she turned and walked out through the revolving doors.

I picked up a cheesecake at the grocery store on my way to Kaity's. I pulled into the driveway. The big five-bedroom, two-story house her mother had left was in one of the more residential neighborhoods.

I walked through the hallway, where a dozen random pictures of Kaity hung on the wall in no particular order. A zesty smell of something Italian wafted from the kitchen, and I followed it.

Kaity smiled when I set down the cheesecake. "Yummy," she said, setting down a pasta dish.

"I didn't know you could cook," I said, checking out the kitchen. The counters shined from top to bottom. "It's really clean here."

Kaity laughed. "My mother liked a clean house, and with her sickness, I tended to do most of it. I don't have much to do during the day, so when I get up, I usually clean. It's kind of like a habit now."

I sat on one of the island stools where she had laid out the spread. She passed me a plate, and we spent the next minutes dipping out chicken parmesan onto our plates. The first bite melted in my mouth.

"You're going to have to teach me this," I said, wiping my mouth with a napkin. "I've been living on frozen microwave dinners or end up having to buy the demons' dinners."

"Lose at cards?" Kaity laughed.

I smiled too. "Yeah, and if I didn't know any better, I'd think they were cheating, but cheating at go fish is childish."

"I know what you mean. I used to go over there after

my mother passed, and they were always winning. I don't know how Luke puts up with it."

"Oh, that's easy. He hardly ever comes out of his room unless he's out patrolling. He does come out for some food, but not all the time," I said, taking another bite.

"They're honestly not bad . . ." Kaity shrugged. "Demons, I guess. Chase and Scout are a funny duo, and Bob makes a mean drink."

I got up and rinsed my plate in the sink, leaving it there, and bit my bottom lip. *What does she think of me dating a demon?*

I faced Kaity and asked, "You didn't seem surprised that Christo and I are dating?"

"I saw you two at dinner a few weeks ago. I think you make a cute couple, but . . ." She paused. "He doesn't seem like your type."

My type? I leaned back against the counter, opening my mouth to ask her what my type was, but she continued before I could ask.

"You know, Christo seems like an f-boy, and you just seem like you're more of the Prince Charming type."

I'd never really dated that many men.

"What's the difference?" I asked.

She lightly tapped her chin. "One will help if asked, but the other one already knows you need him."

Oh. I wonder what type of man Kit is? "Maybe my type is changing."

Kaity raised her eyebrow at my statement but didn't comment.

I eyed the cheesecake, but I was too full. "How are we going to practice when I feel like I'm going to explode?"

Kaity smirked as she brought her plate to the sink. "I guess we could just sit and talk for a little bit. We haven't had much of a chance to chat during our patrols together."

"You're right. Sometimes I wonder why there are so many vampires in the world. Happy Valley seems to be drawing all of them here. I hardly saw any in Berkeley."

"Hmm," she mused, washing her plate. "There used to be a missing person once every ten years, and now there's one every few months. It's unfortunate people still refuse to abide by the curfew that was set a few years ago."

"Yeah, it was the same at Berkeley. Not many cared that the curfew existed. They allowed the students a little bit more leniency, but when they ran out of alcohol, students would still end up leaving and disappearing."

"Wow, so Berkeley had a curfew?"

I sipped my water. "It was established back in the fifties after one hundred people went missing in one week. They haven't changed it since."

Bringing up Berkeley had me thinking about the dress. I still had no way to get there on time. I didn't want to call in sick since I was on thin ice with my boss for coming in late a handful of times already.

"What's up?" Kaity asked, reaching her hand across the island to lie it on mine. "You look deep in thought."

My best friend didn't trust me, and I didn't know if

Dad would ever accept me. But I stuck with the most pressing issue. "I need to get to Berkeley on Friday before five to pick up a dress. But I have to work in the morning. There's no way to make the thirteen-hour drive."

"That's easy," Kaity said.

How so?

"I can take you. It'll only take a few seconds for us to travel there and back."

My hand dropped onto the island with a smack, making me jump at the sound. "You'd do that?"

Kaity's agreeable smile greeted me. "Sure, no problem."

"That would be awesome."

Kaity stared out the windows for a second and then back at me. "Maybe we could stay the night? I've never left Happy Valley."

I was silent for too long, and she started to backpedal, saying it was no big deal.

I assured her, "No, we can totally stay the night. My old college roommate is in her last semester, and we should be able to stay with her on campus."

"Really?" Kaity clapped her hands together.

"You've really never left Happy Valley?"

"My mother was too sick to travel. I did go with everyone to Rabon's house, but that's it."

"I'm so sorry." I squeezed her hand. "But what about now? Your mother is gone, and you have this amazing power that can take you anywhere in the world."

Her eyes widened. She hadn't thought to use her magic for that.

"I guess I can. I wasn't really taught to use my magic to travel like that. But maybe I will. And now I have friends to go with." She smiled at me, happiness written across her face.

"That would be fun," I said.

Kaity was becoming a really good friend to me too. *Better than Grace?*

"Now, we need to practice."

She grasped one of my hands, and when I opened my eyes, we were at the range. It was wide open and secluded. It was always safer to practice our magic in the open air instead of the school's gym. We practiced for about an hour before I headed home to prepare for patrol.

Thirty-six

EMBER

I headed back to Kaity's after work on Friday. Everything had all worked out. Luke had extended our rest week into two so we could go on our girls' night.

"Hey," I yelled, walking into the house. "Sorry I'm late. I had one aggro grandma show up at the last minute. She stuck around for fifteen minutes before taking her money. Then I still had to count my drawer and log it into the safe."

I walked into the kitchen, where Kaity sat on a stool, a backpack sitting next to her.

"It's okay, I just finished packing." She eyed me. "Where's your bag?"

I turned, showing her my small backpack that just contained one set of clothes. "Here."

"Then let's go!" she said, hauling the big backpack onto her shoulders. She held out her hands, and I took them in mine. "I just need you to get a clear picture of a place on campus that is secluded so we can transport there."

"So, how did you get us to Rabon's on your own?"

"Oh, um, well, since Chris had been there already, he provided me with a detailed image of where I needed to take us."

"I see. A place that doesn't have people . . ."

I thought through all the places I'd visited while on campus, but only one would be empty. I pictured that place clearly, and goose bumps rose on my arms, my body tilting to one side as we moved. In the blink of an eye, I gazed upon a jar of frog remains. I backed up, bumping into a rack holding lab supplies and knocking off towels and boxes of rubber gloves.

"Is this the right place?" Kaity asked, stepping over the mess as she headed for the door.

I followed her out into a lab class full of wide-eyed students. We both paused.

"What were you doing in there?" asked the professor, dressed in a white coat.

"Um," I said, grabbing Kaity's hand and inching toward the door that would lead to the hallway. "So sorry, late for class."

We ran out into the deserted hall.

Kaity gave me a pointed look. "I thought I said it should be empty."

"It was. The last time I was here, it was still mostly burned from my mishap."

"What?" Her eyes held disbelief.

"I didn't burn it on purpose. It was the first year I had

my powers, and I only wanted to burn the eyebrows off this jerk's face."

She smirked. "Did you?"

"Oh ya, as far as I know, they never grew back." Kaity laughed, and I reviewed the campus. "This way." I started off toward the closest bus stop. We waited for a few minutes before one came. We hopped on and took a five-minute ride to Blackwell Hall, where I had spent the four years I'd been here.

We headed across the crosswalk and into the apartment-like residential hall. I'd missed my friends dearly—Vanessa, Evie, and Randy.

"This place is huge," Kaity said.

Once inside, I went to the administration counter, where a plate read Mrs. Heiligenstadt. She was behind the window, looking at her computer screen.

"Hello, Mrs. H."

"Ember." She jumped up and came out of the office to give me a hug. "Vanessa submitted the paperwork for your visit. It's been a while."

"Yeah, staying with Vanessa tonight. Girls' night."

"How fun," she said, going back into her office and laying a clipboard on the counter.

I signed us both in and handed it back to her.

She gave us our badges for the night. "You should try to tell Vanessa to stop scaring away her roommates."

I smiled. "Nessa likes things her own way."

Mrs. H chuckled, and I turned to head up the stairs. Kaity followed me as I went to the room that had been my home while I'd gone here. I knocked on the door and waited for a response. None came. I pushed open the door, knowing Vanessa never locked it unless she was sleeping.

The room normally housed three girls, but it had always been just me and Nessa. She had texted me almost weekly on her search for a new roommate, complaining that she would never be able to replace me. She had already gone through three different people.

"Here it is," I said, coming in and dropping my pack by my old bed. "What do you think?"

Kaity walked into the room, putting her bag on the last remaining bed. "It's big. I thought dorm rooms were small."

"The apartment building was remodeled five years ago. Most of the dorms on campus are similar."

"That's neat." She walked over to the windows and looked out at the aquatics building next door.

On the way out, I gave her a tour of how the building was laid out. There was a large common area in the center of the building on the first floor, and then each level above made up the dorm rooms. Many weekends, students would be in the common area until the wee hours, watching movies or playing music.

I pulled my phone out and sent a message to Nessa, telling her we had made it and would be back later tonight.

"Are you ready to head downtown?" I asked.

Kaity eyed my knife as I pulled it from my bag and placed it in my boot.

"I downloaded the directions to my phone, and I

think it will be a nice long walk. At the very least, you'll get to see some of the city."

Kaity walked with me. "That sounds great."

We headed downtown, stopping whenever a shop caught our eyes. I was surprised I had never set foot in many of these shops even though I'd been here four years.

Turning the last corner, I said, "It should be over there." I pointed it out for Kaity.

I spotted two people walking into the shop. *Grandma Sue?* I pulled Kaity back behind the building, hiding us from view.

Sue Ellington was easily recognizable in her black button-down blouse and straight black full-length skirt. Her gray hair was pulled tightly and smoothed to perfection in a bun on top of her head.

I watched my father's mother go into the store with a younger man in a familiar black uniform. He was facing away from me. I couldn't quite place him this far away.

"Who was that?" Kaity asked beside me when she noticed me watching.

"That was my grandmother."

Kaity smiled at me and then started forward. "Let's go say hi!"

I pulled her back, angling us toward the café that was nearby.

"What's wrong?"

"We don't really get along that well."

"Oh, I'm sorry."

"It's okay. I dealt with it my freshman year." My stomach rumbled as the baked bread aroma floated through the air. "Let's get something to eat and wait for them to leave."

"Sure." Kaity followed me to a table facing the shop.

"It's okay, really," I said, pulling out a menu.

We ordered a midafternoon snack and waited for my grandmother to leave the store.

I remembered the first time I'd tried to visit my grandparents without Dad. "It was my first year here. It was wonderful but also really lonely. I was used to my dad always being around, and while Vanessa helped fill that role, we didn't really become close friends until the end of that first year."

"What happened then?" Kaity asked.

"My grandparents live like missionaries. They traveled all over, but they were here in Berkeley for Christmas that year. My grandfather taught online classes, and, well, I'm still not sure what my grandmother actually does." I paused in thought.

I shrugged. "A week before Christmas, Dad mentioned he was booked solid and that driving home would be a waste of time and money. He said I could have more fun in Berkeley than I would at home. He spoke about how his parents were set up at the RV camp near here. I tracked them down a few days before Christmas and was going to thank them for helping me get my scholarship. I found what I thought were the perfect gifts and headed over."

"That sounds nice."

"I'll never forget their expressions when the door opened and I was standing there." *Disgust. Hatred.*

Dread. Much like the way Dad leers at me now. What's so wrong with me?

"We don't have to talk about this now if it's too painful."

I smiled and continued, "I asked to come into their home. But my grandmother sneered, and with malice in her voice she said, 'No, you weren't invited.' Still, I didn't give up. I handed her the presents I'd bought. And what happened next was like a television drama. I watched her jerk them from my hands and slam the door in my face."

"I'm sorry your family is like that."

"Yeah, because it was an RV, their voices carried. She told my grandfather to put them in the trash. I haven't had reason to speak to them since."

Trying to hide my sadness from Kaity, I sipped the black tea in front of me, half turning to look at the dress shop. Some twenty minutes later, the young man, who I could now see was Kit, stepped out carrying a long, slender box. He held the door, and my grandmother followed him out of the building, the two of them heading toward a parking structure. *What is he doing with her?*

"Ready?" Kaity asked when the pair had walked far enough away to not spot us.

I agreed, and we crossed the street. Madam Boutique —Anita's Curiosities was written across both windows in dark blue lettering, but the strange part was the words written underneath in smaller letters. *Where all your magical needs are in one place.*

I turned toward Kaity, pointing at the small words. "I wonder what that means."

"I don't know," Kaity said. "But it sounds convenient."

She took the three narrow stairs and walked into the store.

I followed her, taking a minute to adjust to the purple lights that ran the length of the store. I took in the number of items in the space. It was packed full of rows and rows of clothes on racks. One side had women's clothes, and the other half had men's. Spying leather pants on the men's side, I took a couple more steps into the room. Behind the men's clothing were adult items. Kaity headed to that section as I looked around for an employee. A cash register sat at the back of the room. I went to grab Kaity, only to find her staring up at an interesting device with a curious gaze.

"Have you ever seen anything like this?" she asked. Before I could respond, she added, "What is this?"

Glancing at the item Kaity pointed to, I said, "I'm not sure I want to know."

"It's a holster that straps around your leg," said someone from behind.

We turned to find a woman in her late fifties standing there.

"It's for a weapon like a sword or gun."

I never would have guessed that was the purpose of the item by the way it had been packaged.

"Hello. I'm the one who called about the dress."

The woman eyed me, scanning up and down and nodding. "I can see your mother in your eyes and your father in your face." She turned to go toward the back.

I left Kaity to follow the woman.

She veered left. "There's a dressing room in the back there." She pointed to the closed-off curtain area. "I can make any adjustments if necessary." She pulled back the curtain. "Do you plan to wear it soon?"

"Yes."

Walking into the dressing room, I saw a metallic dark purple dress hanging against the back wall. It had a formfitting corseted bodice and was made out of something I'd never felt before. It had silk straps that would lay over the edge of my shoulders. The bottom of the dress was layers of free-flowing silk.

"I'll be outside when you need help," the lady said, closing the curtain.

Slowly taking my clothes off, I moved to put on the dress. The back closed with tiny buttons, and I would definitely need help to secure them. I moved the curtain aside to see the older lady waiting for me. I turned my back to her, holding still as she buttoned me up. Once done, I stepped farther out. Running my hand down the bodice to the cascading silk, I couldn't keep the tears at bay. It was so beautiful, but my mother never got to wear it.

"Do you not like it?" the lady asked as she stepped around in front of me. "It needs to be altered here and there." She pinched the fabric above my right thigh and at my waist. "You're just a little slimmer than your mother."

"Do you think you'll be able to have that done by tomorrow? We're only in town until noon."

The lady assured me she could. "This here." She

indicated a section of the skirt. "It folds back and buttons so that your legs have more freedom. Your mother always wanted to be sure she was never restricted in a fight. Always prepared, she was."

Always prepared. What happened that day?

"Dear." The shopkeeper's voice faded back in. "Do you need help taking it off?"

I nodded and once again presented my back. The lady worked quickly, and I'd barely caught it when it slipped down my shoulders. I murmured my thanks before reentering the dressing room.

Kaity brought us here for a girls' night out, but in my current mood, I wouldn't provide a great time. I took my time getting dressed to compose myself.

When I came out, the older lady was leaning on the register, listening to Kaity talk animatedly. I came into a conversation centered on herbs.

Kaity leaned sideways and gave me a big smile. "Guess what! Anita had goldenseal. I could only find it on Amazon, and it was never this fresh."

Having no clue what she was talking about, I grinned at Kaity's contagious smile. "I left the dress hanging in the dressing room."

After deciding on a pickup time, Kaity paid for her herbs and we started out of the shop.

"Dear, you may want this." She held out a business card.

I thanked her and read the only two words on it: *Magic Tattoos.* Flipping it over, I checked the back, but it was blank. I said thank you once more before following Kaity out.

The door clicked behind me. "What did she give you?"

I held it out to Kaity.

"Magic Tattoos. Did you tell her you're in need of an artist?"

"Nope," I said, stuffing it into my pocket.

We both shrugged.

We headed back to campus, agreeing to take a new route to see the sights. "My friend Lyra lives down this way. If she's home, we can stop and say hi. She lives in a part of town where all the houses are historical landmarks."

Thirty-seven

LUKE

I stood outside the nurse's station. Ember left earlier with Kaity, so I knew no one would be in there. I slipped the note I'd written earlier into the plastic file box next to the door frame. She would find it there eventually.

Is this the right decision? According to Istros's memories, he vowed to protect the royal bloodline. Protecting Ember would lead to breaking the curse. If I was with Rabon, then I could subvert his attacks against Ember, and being near him would hopefully lead to remembering how the curse could be broken.

I walked away before I changed my mind.

I stood at the entrance of the cafeteria. The three stooges had left an hour ago to see a movie. It was their weekly Thursday afternoon jaunt. *I should have played one more game with them. It's too late now. Hopefully I can find forgiveness from them.*

I crossed the kitchen to Bob's office and turned the

knob. *Locked.* I let loose a breath and twisted the handle. It clattered to the floor. Pushing open the door, I stepped into the room. His desk sat against the back wall and was where he kept the maps of the tunnels for travelers. I opened the drawer where I'd seen the maps and took one, stuffing it into my upper jacket pocket.

I needed one other item—an exclusive ticket for a secret underground train system run by an eccentric billionaire gun manufacturer from California. It would be the fastest way to get me to my destination, and once I stepped on the train, I'd be untraceable. I started moving papers and folders out of the way while I scanned the drawers. But I could sense the sun was going down, and I needed to start my journey. *Where did Bob hide you?* I glanced up at the filing cabinet, staring at a dark jug labeled Rob's Margarita Mix. I grabbed and pulled it down, twisting the cork off the top. The smell of alcohol hit my nose, but it had been drunk long ago.

I peered into the tiny hole, and there was definitely something inside. I smashed the jug onto the floor. Swiping away the broken pieces of glass, I smiled at my prize.

My golden ticket. I bent to retrieve it and stepped away from the mess. *Shit, this is bad.*

I swiped the papers and folders off the desk onto the floor. When I knocked over the lamp, it flickered but stayed on. I flipped the chair upside down before eyeing the bobbleheads on Bob's desk. I picked up the one of Mickey Mantle and pulled the head off. I backed away from the room and against the door when shuffling could be heard coming through the kitchen.

"What are ya doing in here?"

I slid the ticket up my sleeve and turned to face Bob. "I saw that the doorknob was broken and wanted to check it out." I gestured around the room. "Looks like someone broke in."

"Aye, sure does," Bob said, stepping aside as I moved past him.

"I have to run an errand, let me know if anything is missing." I waved, walking through the kitchen. "Sorry, man."

Thirty-eight

EMBER

Even though I grew up in Happy Valley, Berkeley and Lyra's house had truly become a home to me. I walked alongside Kaity, trudging up the hill that would take us there.

"You know," Kaity said. "You don't have to continue living at Parker Elementary if you don't want to. There's more than enough room at my place."

I reached out and stopped her, reading her eyes and knowing she meant those words. "I . . . I never considered it."

Kaity shrugged. "I mean, if you like living there, then don't worry about it. I just thought an actual bed and a room would be more comfortable. Though, I'm going to have to ask you to pay a little rent, not much, since I'm only working part time at Eats! I could use the help with the bills."

I bit my lip. "I understand, and I'll think about it. I

just need to clear up this mess with Dad first. I'm still hopeful he'll want me around."

"Well, in case you don't want to move back in with your father, my door is always open."

With Dad's harsh words and Grace's aversion to demons, I was thankful for Kaity's offer. "What do you think about Chris and I dating?" I asked as we started off again.

I wasn't sure why it mattered, but I really wanted to know her opinion.

She didn't look at me when she answered. "Only you should choose who you date." She captured my eyes. "I mean technically, Luke is also a demon. And I want to be with him, heart and soul." She paused. "He's an assassin. Are you afraid because he's a demon or a killer for hire?"

Stopping again, I swiveled to Kaity. "No. I don't think he would ever hurt me. But he doesn't really talk about what he does. We spend most of our time *cuddling*." I wiggled my eyebrows.

Kaity's eyes went wide before she giggled. "You've been dating long enough."

I sighed. "Seriously though, he's super sweet, but I know he's keeping a lot of secrets from me. And I can't talk to Grace because she thinks all demons are evil. Do you think they're all evil?"

"All men are evil," someone said from up ahead.

I turned to see Lyra standing at her gate.

"I'm right. You should swear off *all* men." She laughed.

"Lyra, meet Kaity." I put my hand on Kaity's shoulder. "Kaity, this is Lyra."

"Hello," Kaity said, striding up to the black wrought iron gate Lyra leaned against. "It's so nice to meet you. Ember talks about you all the time."

Lyra rolled her eyes at me. "You girls got time to come in?" she asked.

"Um . . ." I looked up at the fading light. "Our walk took longer than I thought, and it's almost curfew. We need to check in at the dorm since I registered our names earlier."

Lyra huffed. "I understand, but you could have stayed with me."

I smiled at Lyra. It would likely be a better girls' night for Kaity if we stayed in the dorms where alcohol and boys were free flowing. I was pretty certain she hadn't really gotten to be a regular teenager or ever really drank before.

"Next time we're in town, we'll stay longer," I said, glancing at the house behind her.

"Whoa, is that your house?" Kaity asked, peering past Lyra at the white Victorian with black shutters. "It's super cute."

Lyra wrinkled her nose at the word cute. I wasn't sure why she did that, but she had that reaction anytime the word was used.

"It is cute," I replied to Kaity and hid a laugh with a cough when Lyra wrinkled her nose again.

"Thank you. I bought it in the early twenties," Lyra said with a higher-pitched voice.

I turned to look at her. Did she mean to actually reveal that the house was bought in the 1920s? There was so much mystery surrounding her. Kaity must not have noted the wording because she continued to chat about the style of the house.

Is Lyra an Immortal Demon? Like Christo? They lived long lives, and though Lyra's power was different from Chris's, she only seemed to have one. It had always creeped me out. One millisecond, she would be standing in front of me, and the next, she would be behind.

The women had continued to admire the house until Lyra turned to me. "You better get going, girls, to make curfew. All who go bump in the night could end up a prize for the Cross tonight."

Kaity laughed at Lyra's words. I waved bye as we walked along the sidewalk. We admired the old houses until we hit the campus.

"She knows what goes bump in the night?" Kaity whispered, and I nodded. "So why did she say that?"

I thought about the end of her sentence. *Cross.* My mother had mentioned them in her journal before. "Well, I didn't tell her you were a witch. Maybe she thought you were a human with no knowledge of the supernatural community."

"Oh well, that makes sense. What is she?"

I shrugged. "I don't know for sure. She seems to know a lot about the Zodian powers. Her comment about buying that house in the twenties is strange because she's so young."

Kaity shook her head. "The house has great cosmic energy."

Glancing at Kaity, I stumbled on a loose block of sidewalk. Catching myself, I added, "I didn't know that. I've been in that house many times before and always felt better for some reason, even if I'd had a bad day beforehand."

"I'm not sure what she's doing to maintain the energy there, but it would definitely put someone in a good mood, maybe even give your powers more strength."

"It's crazy really. She owns six other houses. Her favorite house is located in the hills of Kentucky, but I've never been there."

"So, what do you think she is?" Kaity repeated her question.

"I've always thought she was a Zodian, but her powers don't fit with Zodian elemental powers. But maybe she's like Christo."

"Like him in what way?"

I cringed but kept going. "He'll live an extremely long life."

"I've heard of a demon group like that, but I can't remember what they're called."

Not wanting to give away any more secrets about Chris, I was relieved to see we had made good time getting back to the dormitory complex. We waited in the line of students signing in for the night.

"This is crazy."

"Yep, every student is supposed to check in for

curfew. Then, each of the admin staff emails the other dorms with the names of the missing students, and they cross reference. It has always been encouraged that if you couldn't make it back to your own room, to check in at another building."

Kaity leaned into me. "Do you think the college knows what goes bump in the night?"

"It's possible. But I've never seen vampires on campus," I said, whispering the word vampires. "But it would make sense that they knew."

We walked into the entryway, and Mrs. H marked us off the list. After heading up to the room to store Kaity's purchases away, we went down to the common area with the rest of the students. *It's good to be on campus again.*

The sun had set twenty minutes ago, and Vanessa had yet to show up. I checked my phone to read the incoming message I'd missed from her.

VANESSA

I'm at Byran's house. Sorry. I didn't make it back in time. Lunch tomorrow? xoxo

I put my phone in the back pocket of my jeans. A scream broke through the chatter of the room. I stood up like everyone else who heard it, and surveyed the room for the threat.

Someone hollered from the front windows, "Sydney's in trouble!"

"She needs help!" another girl screamed.

I pushed through the throng of students to peer out the window. A young girl was running for her life toward the building. Six pursuers followed closely behind and would overtake her any moment. I pushed the aether out through the doors and across the pavement to find the sour stench of vampires.

Thirty-nine

EMBER

I raced through the crowd toward the exit but skidded into another body. We grabbed each other for balance. The person I locked eyes with was Kaity.

"You ready?" we said in unison.

She smiled at me. We dropped our arms and headed out the glass doors.

Kaity sprinted past the young student and engaged the first vampires.

"Keep running, don't stop until you're in the building," I yelled, passing her. I came to a stop behind Kaity. "We need to move out of view of the dorms. Head toward the stadium."

She peered ahead with a nod and counted down—*three, two, one.* She sprinted through the vampires. I followed her, knocking one down, making sure to piss them off enough to give chase. We didn't stop until we jumped the fence and entered the dark stadium. We hid in an alcove, waiting.

The bloodsuckers slowed to a stop in search of our scent. Their smiles grew, some laughing, most likely thinking we were easy meals. It was unfortunate that we weren't dressed in our usual slaying attire. Especially Kaity. She had decided to wear a mid-length green dress with leggings underneath. But it didn't stop her. Her arms were up, ready to defend herself, like a fierce Amazonian warrior.

I'd dressed in my usual jeans, but instead of my tight jacket, I'd chosen to wear a bright pink sweater. It stood out in the darkness, and I tried to stay hidden until the last minute. I pulled my mother's dagger from my boot.

Their voices grew distant, and I nudged Kaity. We took off in the opposite direction we knew they had gone. But in the darkness, the halls all looked the same, and we ended up sprinting down a long tunnel that led to the field.

"Wrong way," Kaity said.

She turned, but before we knew it, they had herded us into the center of the stadium. Kaity and I took up a stance with our backs to each other. Six vampires meant three for each of us.

Kaity and I moved as one, which reflected the amount of times we had been paired and practiced together over the last few months. Kaity brought her magic forth, taking two down quickly. Sidestepping one moving in from the right, I slashed my mother's dagger at the one in front of me. The vampire to my left took off after Kaity, who was chasing another.

I eyed the two in front of me. They smirked. I lunged

at the closest one, cutting him deep. The sour blood seeping from the wound turned my stomach.

The fiend grabbed my arm, pulling me closer, but it seemed to forget I wielded a pointy object. I plunged it where his dead heart rested.

"Not wood," he sneered, pulling my hand back and freeing the dagger.

He gasped, clutching his chest, and burst into dust.

"Ember!" Kaity yelled.

I turned to see three new ones had joined the chase.

I dispatched another with a quick thrust to his heart. He didn't see it coming. I raced over to help Kaity. One of them had managed to grab hold of her. I punched him, and he released Kaity.

I tried to stab him in the heart, knowing I couldn't miss the cold dead organ. He twisted away from my blade and gripped my arm, thrusting me away. I skidded back, using the air to balance me, and rushed him again. This time I summoned the flames with my blade hand.

Fingers wrapped around my wrist. I turned to stare into Kit's emerald eyes, and I let my fire dissipate.

The moment seemed suspended in time. They sparkled in the dim light.

He pulled me closer, but Kaity's scream broke me out of my trance. I glanced behind me, my hand still clutched in his. Men dressed in black combat uniforms, similar to Kit's, had surrounded Kaity and were throwing powder at her. She shielded her face, stumbling around as if she was drunk, before she collapsed onto the grass.

"Kaity," I yelled, pulling free from Kit's grasp.

I rushed toward her only to catch a face full of the powder. Everything went black.

Forty

KIT

I wasn't fast enough to save her this time. There was nothing I could do but watch as she crumpled to the dirt after inhaling the canceling herbs. *She's so strong. I lost my grip.* When I'd caught her hand and she let her fire die down, I'd hoped none of my men had seen it.

"We better get these two back before they wake up," a soldier said to my left.

I crossed over to him, putting my palm on his chest, stopping him. I lowered my eyes to his and reduced the volume of my voice. "They are not a threat. Leave them. They were fighting the vampires just like us."

"Not for you to decide, sir," he said.

"It's my unit. My say."

The soldier shook off my hand. Others started to notice the tension coming from us.

"The director has final say," he uttered, looking

very interested in this pair." He brushed past me. "Load them up."

I turned and watched as the men gathered Ember's friend into their arms. When they started to do the same to Ember, I couldn't stop myself from shoving them away from her. Picking her up, I cradled her against my chest and followed my unit out of the stadium. *What am I gonna do now?*

The purr of the SUV rumbled through the streets of Berkeley as we made it to the outskirts of town where the Scarlet Cross Church sat. Ember was tucked into my lap. I wasn't about to trust anyone else with her. It was odd to have her this close and not yelling insults at me. Her breathing was shallow, but she was warm and safe for now.

We entered the gates and followed the circle drive. The director stood waiting on the steps with a sour look on her face. *The bastard called ahead.*

We exited the vehicles, but I stayed near the back.

"Kitley," director's high-pitched voice rang out.

Fuck me. A half second later, I'd obeyed the command. Her eyes widened at the sight of Ember in my arms.

She mumbled, "Finally."

"Director," I replied, bowing my head in respect.

"Hand that thing off to someone else. I want a detailed report."

The soldier from the stadium stepped up. "We caught these two." He dragged Ember's friend through the gravel. "They were fighting with the vampires we were chasing."

The director pursed her lips. "Kitley."

Another soldier came up and tried to take Ember from me. When I didn't immediately hand her over to him, he gave me a puzzled look. I relented, passing her limp body over to the man. He carried her off. I watched until they rounded the corner headed for the pit.

I went in to give my report. The son of a bitch followed along. He'd been aiming for my position. I explained clearly the events that occurred throughout the day. The asshole piped up and took over the report of the stadium incident, making sure to note my comments to the director.

"Harris, leave," the director hissed behind her desk.

I bowed, waiting for approval. I stayed still with my eyes cast down, but I couldn't stop myself from speaking. "Ma'am, I don't think those two are a threat. There's no need to send them to the pit. We could use their—"

"Silence."

I tensed at her command.

"Have you forgotten who killed your parents?" she asked. "These things are manipulators. They cannot be trusted. They *will* use you and destroy you from the inside out. They are balaur spawn." She spit onto the floor and rose to her full height. Her palms pressed flat against the desk as she leaned over it, glaring at me with her teeth exposed. "We are losing our world to these monsters. They have taken pieces of my family and yours. How could you sympathize with such evil?"

I fell to my knees. "Forgive my insolence."

The director walked around the desk to stand before me, the blacks of her shoes peeking out from her skirt. The smell of starch and polish enveloped the space around me. She laid her hand on top of my head. "You, Kitley, are my brightest and greatest accomplishment. Out of two hundred, you have come out on top and earned your place as my second. It would be unfortunate for you to fall from my graces. Rise."

I rose, towering above her.

She looked me in the eye. "You'll release all your doubts tonight at the pit. There is no mercy for evil."

Ember isn't evil. My fingernails dug into my palms behind my back.

"One hour, and I'll show you how to deal with balaur," she said, waving her hand dismissively.

The darkness that consumed me still lingered in the back of my mind. *I have to wake up.* I sat cross-legged in a wide expanse somewhere deep in my subconscious. My body felt heavy. Shadows swirled around me, nipping at my skin like the bite of frozen air. I breathed in the chill but exhaled flames. Encasing myself in light and fire, I destroyed the darkness that tried to engulf me.

My eyes snapped open. Bright light flooded my vision, blinding me. My eyelids closed involuntarily. I wanted to shield them. But my hands were numb, tied above my head. My sweater was hiked up my back, and the splinters of the wood post dug into my skin. My feet were secured to the base. I couldn't move my legs.

"Ember!"

Kaity's panicked voice came from behind me. It sounded small, like she was terrified, but I couldn't remember a time I'd ever seen her afraid of anything, except losing Luke. She'd always rushed headlong into any challenge.

I squinted, searching below the bright lights. My eyes slowly adjusted. "What happened?" Glancing up, I tested my restraints. All around us, charred wood and ashes were scattered. We were tied to a post on a newly constructed wooden platform. Four stadium lights spotlighted us in the center of the field. *What is going on?*

"I don't know," she said, her voice barely above a whisper. "My powers are gone."

She was desperate.

I tried to see her face when her voice cracked, but the ropes were unyielding. It sounded like she was on the verge of tears.

"It's okay. We'll figure this out."

"Is there any way you can connect with Lyra?" Kaity asked.

I considered the idea. "Not that I know of."

"Shit! How are we going to get out of this?"

The aether caressed my senses. I looked around instantly, pushing it out farther and drawing it back in. It was a relief to know that my powers were working even if Kaity's weren't. But the aether also told me someone I knew was here with us, watching our exchange.

Kit stepped into the circle of lights shining down on us. He brought his hand up, holding a small device, and with a push of the button, the lights dimmed.

I met those emerald eyes that stared back at me, *but* they were not twinkling like earlier.

My temperature rose under his gaze. "What the hell is going on?" I hollered.

"Why are you doing this?" Kaity shouted.

Kit bit his lip and took a deep breath. "You are balaur spawn, and it is my commitment to cleanse this world of your evil."

The tears built in my eyes. *How could he believe that about me?* I had no words.

"What the fuck did you do to us?" Kaity screamed.

Being stripped of her magic was having a powerful effect on her.

He stood silent and glanced behind him for a second before answering Kaity's question. "The powder you both inhaled has the ability to nullify your powers. For a short time." He whispered the last four words.

Kaity tensed behind me. The ropes tightened around us.

I whispered to her, "It's just for a short while. You'll get them back."

Kaity addressed Kit. "You could help us get out of here."

His eyes locked with mine, and his face dropped. He walked away back into the shadows, leaving us alone.

"Is he going to help?" she asked.

I held my breath but knew she figured it out. "He left."

"Fuck. Come back and help us," Kaity yelled.

"It's okay, Kaity." I tried to ease her worry by reaching my fingers to rub the side of her hands.

"What are we going to do?" she whispered.

"I've got you." My powers still worked, and I would make sure we got out of this unscathed.

"You still have your—"

I cut off her, whispering, "People are watching."

I had let the aether follow Kit into the shadows, where it alerted me there were more than thirty people gathered around us.

"I am so glad you could finally join us," said a woman.

Kaity gasped behind me as my grandmother walked out of the shadows.

Several pieces fell into place. My grandparents had never liked me because my mother had been a Zodian, and now I was choosing to follow her path. "Why are you doing this?"

"Emma."

I leaned forward, seething. "My name is Ember."

The rope securing me held me back and caused more abrasions on my wrist.

Grandmother Sue cackled. "Awe, I hit a nerve. I'm the one who gave you that name, you ungrateful spawn of evil." She faced the crowd surrounding us and called out, "Come closer."

Those gathered swarmed around us before focusing back on her.

"Who the fuck are you people? What is happening?" Kaity asked, not being able to see what was happening in front of me.

The gatherers had begun passing out torches.

"I'm sure you've heard of us. We are *the Scarlet*

Cross. You will burn." Sue Ellington was handed a torch, and she stepped forward, lighting the base below our platform.

The Cross. Rabon's offhanded comment made sense now. Kitley was part of the Scarlet Cross.

"What?" Kaity screeched. "What the fuck is the matter with you people? You can't do this. It's murder. It's barbaric!"

I agreed and remembered parts of my mother's journal where she referenced the Scarlet Cross as believers of archaic teachings.

Kit stepped forward. "We have a partnership with the authorities."

Kaity began to cry profusely. "How could you even threaten to burn your own family?"

My eyes locked on Kit. His face was stoic, but his eyes shined with intensity. *He didn't know.*

"She's not my family!" Sue spat on the ground, stepping on it and grinding her heel into the soil.

"Awe, did we hit a nerve?" I asked.

She sneered, and her nostrils flared. Her anger was almost palpable as the heat of the fire roaring with more life below us.

"Looks like we have," I mocked.

"You are evil and will die here tonight."

"We are not evil," Kaity cried.

"This world can only be pure when all balaur are destroyed," she spewed, and the congregation cheered.

"Kaity," I said to get her attention. "Kaity," I said it louder. "It's okay. Don't worry. I got this."

"You have nothing, Ember Storm."

I glared at Sue Ellington. *How does she know my mother's last name?* I'd taken it when I decided to keep my powers. Using the aether, I searched for a way out. I gasped, my knees giving out. The ropes bit into my wrists as I slumped against my bonds.

"Em," Kaity said. "Are you okay?"

My dad stood in the shadows, hidden behind the rest of the group. But he was there. He was listening to everything that was happening. *Why isn't he stopping this madness?*

The aether flickered in Kit's direction. He had stepped forward but then retreated. *Does he even care?*

Sue Ellington yelled, "Light them up."

The men holding torches started chanting and came closer, adding theirs to the pyre.

"You can't do this," Kaity pleaded.

The torches were thrown from all directions. Most landed around the edges of the platform, but many reached our feet.

The heat was growing exponentially. I didn't know how long we could last.

"No, please stop," Kaity wailed, pulling and fighting against the ropes.

Dad, stop this, I prayed.

The fire rose, the warmth fast and furious.

He loved me. He raised me; he couldn't let me die here. He had to save us. *Right?*

"Ember," Kaity cried. "Do something."

Sue stepped closer. "Your powers are useless."

I searched for Dad's face within the mob. *Why?* He remained hidden in the shadows, and instead, my eyes found Kit's. Again, his face was emotionless, but his eyes were a beacon in the darkness. His arms were tense at his sides, his hands balled into fists.

"Ember!" Kaity bellowed again.

The flames were rising all around us.

"Kaity." I leaned back so she could hear me over the roar of the flames. "Can you reach my fingers? We need to be touching. Kaity!"

Her fingers brushed against my skin, and I reached for her. We locked three together, but that was enough.

I breathed in the heat, pulling the flames closer to us. It rose above our heads. The Scarlet Cross sank back into the darkness. Kaity's bloodcurdling scream sent a chill up my spine.

I took one shuddering moment as the flames licked at the ropes. The thread disintegrated, and I fell to my knees. Pushing up, I reached over to Kaity, checking her pulse. She was bruised but breathing.

"Kaity," I shook her shoulder, trying to pull her up. "Kaity! You're fine. Snap out of it."

Kaity's eyes met mine, and she jumped into my arms. I gave her a second to recover.

"She warned us," she mumbled into my ear.

"Take my hand. Follow my lead." I grabbed her head to look at me. "Don't let go of me." She nodded, and I continued. "We're going to jump off the platform and find a way out. Ready?"

She nodded again, and I directed the flames around

the platform to form a perfect circle to protect us, keeping the hunters at bay. We took several steps before jumping off the platform in front of us.

Standing, I squared off with Sue Ellington. "We didn't want to burn today."

Kaity squeezed my fingers, huddling behind my frame.

Ellington stepped forward. Flames nipped at her feet, halting her. While she was distracted, I surveyed the area now that the lights weren't blinding me. I couldn't tell in the darkness if they carried any kind of weapons, but the aether told me they were all human.

"How is she doing that?" several members asked. "She was doused with the strongest powder."

I cocked my head, willing the flames to erupt from the ground, striking fear in the members of the Cross. Cries were heard as some of the members fled.

"Where do you think you're going? Get back here!" Sue yelled at her men. "There's no way out, Ember." She turned back to me, cocking her hip out, appearing indifferent.

But her wide eyes frantically scanned back and forth.

How could I have been so wrong? The signs had always been there.

My voice rose over the roar of the inferno. "I see the truth hidden in the shadows. Dad! I know you're out there. How many more secrets are you keeping? How could you love her but not *me?*" I fought to hold back the tears. "Fine. If you don't want me, I don't need to be *your* daughter anymore."

The remaining hunters stood silent, meeting Sue Ellington's eyes, waiting for her instructions.

"Not all supernaturals are evil," I said, tightening my fingers around Kaity's and raising my other hand toward the sky.

Lightning swirled above. Energy buzzed around us, pulling at our feet—crackling.

"Kill her now," Sue screeched, motioning to Kit.

"Just like not all humans are kind and decent. Think about what you are doing here. How many lives will you destroy?"

I found Kit once more, his eyes duller than normal. I summoned the energy.

Anger, hurt, and betrayal grew inside me, and I used those tumultuous emotions to channel Agni. The sky flashed purple, and our hair stood on end. In a breath, the bright light exploded from the ground and carried us to Lyra's.

Forty-two

LUKE

I'd packed light for my journey underground, knowing I wouldn't need anything from that life anymore. After memorizing Bob's map, I followed the different routes that had been carved out of stone. I was making decent time, and depending on how fast the train was to Berkeley, I could be at Rabon's by tonight.

I came around the last corner to find a set of steps leading up. Taking them two at a time, I reached the top landing and was greeted by a metal door stamped with the word Bar across the middle. I tried the handle, but it was locked. I knocked.

A small opening at eye level greeted me, yellow-slitted eyes staring out. "Holy shit."

The small opening closed.

"Hey," I yelled, pounding.

It opened once more. "What do you want?"

"I need passage to Berkeley. I'm told this is where the train stops."

The yellow eyes blinked.

"Is this the right place?"

"Yeah, but the train doesn't come until the wee hours."

"Fine, let me in. I'll wait."

"You'll wait?"

"That's what I said," I huffed. "Let me in." *Before I tear the door off its hinges.*

The demon stood silent on the other side of the door far longer than necessary. "No."

He slammed the small door in my face once more.

"Fuck you."

I brought my foot up and kicked in the center of the door. It gave a little. I kicked again, making it cave in on itself. Several tries later, the door landed with a thud on the floor of the bar. I stepped over it.

The room held a dozen or so demons. Some sipped drinks while a couple played pool. The yellow slit-eyed demon was staring down at the door with his mouth hanging agape.

I headed for a booth. Once I sat down, my arm burned. I shrugged off my coat, noticing the scars I'd received from Ember's lightning were glowing. *Shit.* "Bring me a whiskey, neat."

Forty-three

EMBER

Kaity's scream faded as we landed on our feet, crumpling to the grass. She rolled away from me, patting down her body and hair. When she finally seemed to come out of her fear, she glared at me. "Why am I always catching on fire around you?"

"Sorry," I said, picking myself up off the ground.

I smiled at the familiar sight since we had been here earlier in the day.

"What are you doing here?" Lyra materialized.

Jeez, could she be less creepy?

"What happened? Why are you both covered in burn marks?"

"Because *this* genius thought it would be good to blow us up with lightning," Kaity said, throwing her arms in the air. "Wait, how did we get *here*?" She turned in a circle.

I smiled. "I'll tell you later."

"What happened?" Lyra asked again.

Most of the time she was aloof in her affections, but every once in a while, she went real mama bear on me. I smiled up at her.

"The Scarlet Cross," Kaity yelled, making me shush her. "You warned us."

Lyra nodded, waving us into the house.

"They took my powers." Kaity pouted as she headed in.

"They didn't *take* your powers. Don't you remember what Kit said?" I commented, stepping into the back screened-in porch.

"Oh, you're on a first-name basis with him?"

I whipped my head over to Kaity. *What's her deal?* "No. I just remember his name. He said it was temporary. The effects would wear off."

"That's good news. Man, I smell burnt," she whined.

Lyra laughed, glancing between both of us. "Come with me, Kaity."

I eyed a small chaise lounge at the other end of the porch and sank down onto it, sighing in relief. A sense of peace floated in along with waves of grief. Now that I knew Dad would never forgive me, I could get through this with time.

Lyra appeared and sat down. "Tell me what happened?"

I hadn't heard her come back, but that was usual for Lyra. I sat there a while, not really wanting to talk about it. Kaity and I could have died tonight. The only reason we were alive was because my fire burned through the powder quicker. If they had just stabbed us back at the university, we would have been dead.

"Ember?" Lyra probed, breaking the silence.

My eyes landed on her impassive face. "We made it back to the dorms, but vampires attacked someone, and we went to help. We ended up at the stadium, handling things when the Cross showed up." I buried my head in my hands. "The aether just told me they were humans. If I had known more about them, tonight could have been different."

"What happened then?"

"They threw this crazy powder in our faces, and the next thing we knew, we woke up tied to a stake on a wooden platform. It was terrifying, and more so when Kaity began to panic because her magic was gone."

"But you didn't lose your powers?"

I shook my head. "I did for a short time, but I could feel my fire burn through the drug."

"That's interesting. Their powders affect all supernaturals. You two were very lucky. The Cross hunts supernaturals daily." She shifted in her seat. "Something else happened. You're different now than earlier."

I kept eye contact with her, a mirror reflection of my own violet eyes, before pulling away. "When they had all assembled around us, my dad's mother walked out as the leader." I felt her tense. "After we had words about how I've never been her granddaughter, she told her lackeys to set us on fire. While they were doing that, I knew we would be okay and sent out the aether to see how many we would need to fight to escape."

"And obviously not that many."

"There were thirty or so, but what caught my attention was someone familiar standing in the shadows."

Lyra stood up. "Please tell me he wasn't there."

Whether she knew or not who was there, I didn't know, but I answered anyway. "Dad stood in the back. I held off using my powers because I thought he would jump in to save us."

"He didn't?"

"No. All this time, I've been trying to make him understand how I feel about my powers. All the worry. The self-doubt that's been building. Knowing he will never accept me with my abilities is almost a relief."

Lyra crossed over and pulled me into a hug. She hardly ever touched me or anyone.

"I'm sorry, kid. Families can do some terrible things," she murmured in my ear.

We stayed like that for a while before she pulled me toward the house. "Let's get you to bed."

Forty-four

KIT

I yanked the door of the shop open. *Fucking errand boy now.* I sailed through the aisle, jerking to a stop when Ember stepped out of the dressing room. My breath caught, and my eyes widened.

"Kit," she whispered.

I stood still, scanning her from head to toe. "Yes, me."

A shiver ran down her body, eyes widening. She stepped closer, now only an inch away.

I leaned down to her ear and murmured, "You look amazing."

"Here you are." Anita came out from the back, holding a small rectangle box, and handed it to me.

I accepted it before turning back to Ember. Reaching inside my breast pocket, I pulled out a dagger she would recognize.

"That's mine," she snapped.

I smiled down at her and started to hand the dagger

over but stopped midair. "I found it." Speaking only for her to hear, I said, "I think I'll keep it."

I smirked at her balled-up fists.

"I'll get it back later."

"Is that a promise?"

"You're an asshole."

I walked out, listening to her rage from inside the store.

I was relieved when she walked out of that dressing room. Ember was too tough to die. I knew that. But that hollow pit in my stomach had been there until I saw her. She had smiled slightly before yelling at me. *Seems she missed me too.* She'd been fucking gorgeous in that dress. But last night, standing with the ring of fire around her, eyes alight with fury, she'd been mesmerizing. My heart constricted when the lightning had snapped up from the earth and she'd disappeared.

My childhood nightmares had returned after I'd kissed Ember on New Year's all those years ago. I'd been having more and more, getting worse after she'd disappeared in the cemetery. Not only were they a constant companion, I now saw Ember in them.

I leaned against the brick building a block away from the shop, hiding behind an industrial dumpster, watching Ember and Kaity enter the alleyway across from me to only shimmer out and away, likely back to Happy Valley, once they looked both ways.

Last night I almost stepped in. *She is evil.* I can't spare her again.

Forty-five

LUKE

I stood in the exact same spot I had all those months ago when Rabon held Ember. I clenched my fists. The guards didn't know what to do with me. They whispered that this had never happened before. I'm sure they meant in the various other lives I'd returned from. *Had I never sided with Rabon before?* I wondered if Istros's memories would fully return.

"Brother."

I glanced at the upstairs balcony. Rabon looked down at me with the same smile he wore when he killed.

"What a pleasure," he drawled. "What can I do for you? Come to kill me?" He laughed as if I could actually kill him.

I grinned at him. "Oh no, that's a Tuesday kind of day, and today's Friday."

"Of course," he humphed.

He stood there for a long minute, looking down at me.

Whether he believed me or not, he finally grinned ear to ear. "Well, that's more like it."

"I'm ready to be a god," I said. *Will he believe that?*

"You are one. All you have to do is act like it, and we will rule the world." He clapped his hands together, then waved me up. "Let me show you what I'm planning."

Forty-six

EMBER

Standing in front of the dark house, I'd beat Dad home from Berkeley, of course. The curtains were drawn shut, and there were no lights on anywhere inside.

I walked around the back to stand below my window since I would never have a key again. Instead of climbing up the drainpipe, I pushed air downward, allowing me to levitate, and guided myself up onto the roof. I landed with a soft thump and walked to the window, lifting it one last time.

Standing in my old room filled with boxes, I snapped my fingers, made several fireballs, and tossed them around to light the room. I noted that some of the boxes were now sealed and labeled. I pulled open a box labeled clothes and dug through the sweaters and pants.

Pulling a suitcase from the hall closet, I loaded it with several pieces of clothing I would need. I tried to remember if there was anything else from what I'd found so far: makeup, clothes, hair essentials, and some old journals. Satisfied that I collected all I needed from this life, I sealed the luggage and heaved it out onto the roof. I had decided to move in with Kaity.

Taking the stairs two at a time, I skidded to a stop in front of my mother's picture. *I really shouldn't take it.* As far as I knew, this was the only picture Dad had of Mom. I reached up, touching the frame, hesitating before snapping it off the wall.

I clung to the photo. My father had made his decision. This was mine.

Thank You

Thank you so much for picking up *The Scarlet Cross*, if you enjoyed this story, writing a review would be extremely helpful to me.

Goodreads
Amazon
Barnes and Noble

And if you want to read more about Luke, check out this snippet from his *Lost Chapter* below.

Lost Chapter

LUKE

I stood still and waited for the ten kindergartners to form a line on the mat, trying to keep the smile off my face. A small brunette dressed in a ballerina tutu danced to her place.

Once the students were in a semi-line, I addressed them. "Good afternoon, class." I smiled, opening my arms.

"Hi, Mr. Bowen," yelled some of the kids, kicking their feet or swinging their arms.

One little boy missed another by an inch.

"Let's review what we learned last week?" I paused, scanning the line.

"Um," someone said at the front of the building.

I ran my eyes over a strawberry-blonde girl. She stood with her hands in the back of her jeans, a hip jutted out to one side. A frown formed on her beautiful face.

Someone tugged at my shirt, and I finally opened my mouth to respond. "Yes, can I help you?"

"Is this the boxing class?" she asked.

"Yes. Do you need to sign your child up?"

She bit her lip, chewing it. "No. It's a bit embarrassing, but I wanted to sign myself up."

"Oh," I sighed.

The little girl who tugged on my shirt squeaked at the young lady, "Join us!"

"Oh no, I couldn't."

I skirted around the little ones and grasped her soft hands. "No, join us. It'll be fun."

She gazed up at me with giant sea-glass-green eyes. We stood, clutched together, for what felt like a thousand heartbeats.

"Mr. Bowen?" a wily boy asked.

I let go of her hands. "You in, miss?"

READ THE REST OF THE CHAPTER
BY SIGNING UP FOR MY NEWSLETTER AT
WWW.KASEYLEALMA.COM

Bob's Bloody Hex

1 oz blueberry lemon rum
1 oz triple sec
4 oz pineapple juice
Splash of grenadine

Mix ingredients together and add ice. Drink responsibly.
Take small sips and pace yourself. Trust me on this.

Acknowledgments

I cannot thank my critique partners enough over the last several years! Alyssa, Brittany, and Lana have been with me throughout these first two book launches. When I told the universe I was ready to buckle down and get serious about my writing, they came into my life. They are wonderful, and I just want to thank them from the bottom of my heart for their friendship.

I want to thank my husband for taking on more responsibility during my writing times and always believing I could do this when I didn't.

I want to thank my editor Jeanine for letting me push back my deadlines for both books. She is such a sweetheart and easy to work with.

I also want to thank Erica Abner for helping me whip up the drink mixes that Bob makes for his bar.

Also want to thank the authortube community for getting me excited about writing again.

See you in the next one . . .

About the Author

First, I just want to thank you for continuing to read Ember's story. It means the world to me. Don't worry, I'm working on the next one in between family time with my husband,  two sons, and various four-legged creatures.

I started writing because I was dissatisfied with an ending to a story once, and that was that. I picked up my ballpoint pen and started writing on legal pads. Eventually, I moved to typing, and once the words flowed, magic was created.

Join my community and follow me

www.kaseylealma.com